THIS
CLUB
FROWNS
ON
MURDER

THIS
CLUB
FROWNS
ON
MURDER

ALBERT
BOROWITZ

*For Judy Staud,
with best regards,
Albert Borowitz
2/15/90*

ST. MARTIN'S PRESS • NEW YORK

DESIGN BY BETH TONDREAU DESIGN

Library of Congress Cataloging-in-Publication Data

Borowitz, Albert, 1930–
    This club frowns on murder.
       p.   cm.
    ISBN 0-312-03943-3
    I. Title.
PS3552.07547T4   1990   813'.54—dc20   89-48529

First Edition
10 9 8 7 6 5 4 3 2 1

For the next generation,
Dana, Kate, and Alexandra;

In memory of my father;
and

For my sharp-eyed secretary,
Jami Talliere Toth.

THIS
CLUB
FROWNS
ON
MURDER

PROLOGUE

The University's color was oxblood, and the Alumni
Club in New York City never let you forget it. In the
library on the second floor, two stiffly military ranks of
oxblood leather armchairs stood on an oxblood carpet and
faced each other across a long new-acquisitions table featur-
ing, in slanting built-in racks at each end, books recently
contributed by Alumni authors. On all four walls maho-
gany-stained shelves rose to the ceiling; access to the high
places was furnished by a collection of elephant ladders, the
gift of one of the most eminent American sportsmen of the
nineteenth century.

Only two of the armchairs were occupied at the moment.
A pair of members had just come in together and, as if by
agreement, had placed the greatest distance between themselves that the arrangement of armchairs allowed, one man
taking the first chair to the left of the entrance and the other
the farthest in the opposite row. The long diagonal of carpet,
broken by the hedge of books on the display table, protected
them from conversation and even from introductions. The
librarian was not on duty this afternoon, but his presence was
not needed to maintain silence; the two men had learned
library decorum at the University and that one should not be

impulsively friendly, even to schoolmates. One of the members, a balding, fair-skinned young man with a poorly thriving pink mustache, took a *Wall Street Journal* out of his dispatch case and turned to the stock quotations. The second man, middle-aged and portly, had risen from his chair and, keeping the book table safely between himself and his fellow club member, was examining the graduates' latest literary offerings.

At the far end of the library another door led out onto a gallery overlooking the Great Hall, now sinking into darkness as dusk gathered. Here another member sat apart, at a small writing desk supplied with club stationery and illumined feebly by an old bronze table lamp. On the desk lay a letter just composed in neatly printed capital letters:

Dear Mrs. Richardson,

I do not think you know me, and perhaps it is wrong for me to intrude upon your grief. Still I must let you know how I, and all the members of the Alumni Club, sympathize with you in John's untimely death. It is unnecessary to tell you what a void his passing will leave here. He was one of the most effective presidents the Club has had in my time, and I often cite his example as proof that a man can do a great job in office even when his election has been controversial. I never thought it was fair for his opponents to hold his Watergate involvement against him. John was not indicted on the check-laundering charges, and I'm sure the grand jury carefully considered all the evidence offered by the U.S. Attorney. Besides, as I personally told many of his detractors at the time the Alumni Board vote was announced, it wasn't as if John were being proposed for Club Treasurer.

I do not have to tell you what a warm person John was and how impossible it was to resist his charm. It is true that what his good friends understood to be geniality strangers might mistake for flirtation. We who love him know he did occasionally stumble, but I assure you the rumors you must have heard are overblown.

There was, of course, the Mexican folkloric ballet dancer and the bathing incident at Juan-les-Pins, but after all, as Christopher Marlowe once wrote (wasn't it Marlowe?), that was in another country, and the wench is dead. I don't know why people dwell on this kind of story, and forget all the good things John did, both for the Nixon Administration and the Club.

God bless you in this difficult hour.

A Friend from the Alumni Club

Had the two members in the library cupped their ears they might have heard a low laugh from the direction of the gallery and these muttered words of author's pride:
"I like this one; it's one of my best. Too bad John Richardson isn't dead."

In a meeting room adjacent to the River Suite, where meals were served when the club's main dining hall was filled to capacity, chairman Ralph Murray coughed nervously as he prepared to address the Admissions Committee. So far all had been smooth sailing, but the next few minutes would be tricky.

The current brochure announced that there was no black-balling at the Alumni Club. In the most literal sense, that was quite true. The ancient voting box had been retired to a glass-fronted curio cabinet in the library; the black and white marbles that the committee's predecessors had dropped to approve or condemn applicants had come to rest forever in the box's entrails. But in no other respect had the club's admissions procedures changed in the slightest. The names of candidates were posted on a bulletin board in the foyer, and after the thirty days allotted for the whispering campaigns to run their course, the Admissions Committee met. Two dissents were enough, as they had been for over a century, to defeat an application, but the voting marbles of the past had been replaced by the secret ballot.

Murray jingled some coins in his trousers pocket as he

often did when he was uneasy. As the youthful head of the mergers and acquisitions department of a Wall Street invest-ment banking firm, he was very effective in one-on-one negotiations but was not born to be an orator or politician. "Gentlemen," he began, "you'll recall that when I submitted ten names for approval by acclamation, I told you I would hold back the two remaining candidates for separate consid-eration. For different reasons, their cases are not so easy. I'll ask the Secretary to read the file summary on Thomas Simmons."

Ross Lytton nodded to the chairman and untied the Simmons dossier. The slightly built, stoop-shouldered Lyt-ton was a veteran member of the club staff, a few months away from retirement, who served as secretary of many of its committees. A methodical and unsmiling man, he had mastered the arts of keeping meetings on track and of staying safely away from controversy or commitment. As a result of his prudence, his face remained unlined and he had only a scattering of gray hairs to show for his sixty-odd years. After reading Simmons' academic credits and describing him vaguely as a "self-employed venture capitalist," Lytton came to the heart of the matter.

"Mr. Simmons has been sponsored for nonresident mem-bership by one of the University's most distinguished grad-uates, the poet Jack Feldman. Mr. Simmons' recent years, as is well known, have been a mixture of tragedy and triumph. In 1980, he shot and killed his socially prominent wife Evelyn in their suburban Philadelphia home. Despite his claim that he had been cleaning his .44-caliber magnum in preparation for the hunting season and that it had accidentally misfired, the jury, after lengthy deliberation, found him guilty of voluntary manslaughter, a verdict many observers regarded as a compromise. While incarcerated, he wrote a moving indictment of the Pennsylvania prison and parole systems. Published under the title *Spewed Out,* Simmons' book won him the Pulitzer Prize and the plaudits of many of America's leading writers, including Jack Feldman. It is Feldman who led the fight for Simmons' early release and now proposes his admission to the club."

Lytton had finished reading and stared into space.

"The floor is open for discussion," the chairman said, turning slightly to expose his finely drawn profile, as he was accustomed to do when he feared words might fail him. His bridgeless nose remained Classic Greek, but the jaws were going soft from too many banquets celebrating too many takeover victories.

"Frankly, I think the jury was too easy on him," a member commented. "He hadn't been hunting for five years, and he inherited over ten million dollars."

"Come on, John," protested his neighbor. "We're not here to retry the Simmons case, I hope, or to argue about Jack Feldman's poetry, for that matter, or his choice of causes."

A third member joined the debate. "Richard's absolutely right. Let's stick to the subject. As far as I'm concerned, this man has served his time. What did they use to say in the old movies? He's paid his debt to society. If he comes highly recommended, that's good enough for me, unless there's something in the rule book against taking in felons. What do the rules say, Lytton?"

"The matter is left to the committee's discretion, Mr. Kennedy. The bylaws stipulate only that the candidate must have received a degree from the University or have studied there for at least one academic year as an undergraduate or in a graduate program, or have performed a special service to the University. Apart from that, eligibility is governed by the rules of this committee."

"And what do the committee rules add?" Brian Kennedy, an advertising executive, asked with a hint of irony.

"Nothing much, I'm afraid, sir. As you know, they require the proposer to arrange appointments for the candidate to visit at least two members of the Admissions Committee. The file indicates that these interviews have taken place successfully."

Kennedy smiled and scratched his long jaw. "So there's

nothing to indicate that murder disqualifies a candidate; in other words, that murder's against the club rules?"

Murray glowered at Kennedy; every committee seemed to have its self-appointed jester. He intervened to cut off further conversation.

"Does that about cover it, gentlemen? If so, we're ready for a vote." Ross Lytton distributed ballots around the table. Brian Kennedy, as he waited for his ballot, counted the members who were present. They were twelve, including the chairman. Just the number of Simmons' jury.

A few moments later Lytton recircled the table, collecting the votes. He returned to his seat at the chairman's side, and examined the ballots with an exaggerated show of care. He then whispered a few words to the chairman. "Gentlemen," Murray announced, "the candidate is admitted."

Some of the members were beginning to look at their watches; the committee meetings rarely lasted more than half an hour and there was an unwritten law that adjournment would come in time for one or two drinks and an early train to Westchester. Murray felt, as had many of his predecessors, that this tradition kept the chairman out of harm's way, and he turned once again to the secretary. "Mr. Lytton, if you will, we are ready to hear the summary of Ben Tolliver's application."

Ben Tolliver was a faculty applicant. The owner of three degrees from the University, he had recently been appointed assistant professor in the English Department, where he taught the freshman survey course and a seminar on Shakespeare's contemporaries.

It was when the rate of Lytton's speech slowed slightly and his usual monotone was replaced by a marked singsong that the secretary's listeners knew that he was getting to the meat of the report: "None of the commentators questions in the slightest the brilliance of Professor Tolliver's intellect or the strength of his attachment to the University both as a student and more recently as a member of its faculty. Certain members, however, have expressed some doubt concerning his personal integrity or, to put the matter in better focus, his reputation for personal integrity. These qualms aside, the principal reservation most often presented in response to the posting of this nomination relates to the applicant's life-style."

"Just what is it that is meant by 'life-style' in this instance?" drawled a short leonine man between puffs on his meerschaum. His name was Victor Baines; he was an executive with an important charitable foundation and always felt it his duty to search out possible community concerns, wherever they might lurk.

Murray indulged the chairman's prerogative of wincing visibly. "I think we all know perfectly well, Vic, what our files mean by 'life-style.' In your line of work, you must be only too aware of the equal-rights ordinances that have been adopted in this city and of others that may be tossed into the hopper. But to spell it out for you, Professor Tolliver is widely thought to be a homosexual."

"And is that the end of the report?" asked another member.

Murray, with a parliamentary hand gesture, yielded to Lytton. "That's all the summary says," Lytton replied curtly.

A moment of silence intervened while Murray and several others wondered what to do next. This left the floor open for Brian Kennedy, who was never hampered by such doubts. "Gentlemen, let's confess what many of us are thinking: that the authors of this file are indulging in a bit of self-censorship. Everyone who reads the University *Oxblood* (that is, everyone who reads more than the discouraging sports news) will remember something about the Tolliver affair. But let me remind us all that when Tolliver was still an instructor he was the subject of sexual harassment charges brought by an undergraduate male student. The student claimed he'd asked for counseling following a disappointing exam score and was invited by Tolliver to call at the teacher's rooms. Much to the student's embarrassment he found the walls of the apartment covered with series photographs of frontal male nudes. Before he could recover from this first shock, he says Tolliver propositioned him. The student asserted that he immediately left the apartment in indignation and that afterwards, despite redoubling his efforts in Tolliver's course, he received an F, the only failing grade he had ever received in college."

"I must be behind in my class dues," said the fund-raiser Baines, "my *Oxblood* subscription has been discontinued. What happened next?" He had deposited his extinct pipe in an oxblood ashtray and ran his fingers through his graying theatrical locks.

Kennedy waited for Murray's permission to continue; the chairman nodded reluctantly.

"The complaint was submitted to a combined faculty-student committee and was found to be completely groundless. The most that the hearing panel found was that Tolliver and the student had a strong disagreement about photographic art. Tolliver was fully exonerated and, as Lytton told us, was ultimately appointed an assistant professor. The final irony is that Tolliver's student flunked out of the University two years later. Maybe Tolliver's only fault was seeing the handwriting on the wall—I can't seem to get Tolliver's wall out of my mind—before his colleagues were able to do so. Have I summarized the situation correctly?"

A question seemed poised on Baines's lips but never emerged. Kennedy scanned the table for a moment; nobody in the room was heard to contradict him, and no wonder, cocktail hour was tantalizingly close.

At last Kennedy turned to the secretary. "I will ask Mr. Lytton whether there is anything in the club rules against the admission of homosexuals."

Lytton shook his head while the chairman favored Kennedy with his best approximation of a baleful stare.

"If there is no further discussion," Murray said, "I will call for delivery of the ballots."

Lytton made the distribution. The committee voted in silence and Lytton passed around the table again to pick up their ballots. His review of the votes seemed to take a little longer this time but after a few moments he whispered the result to Murray. Expressionlessly the chairman reported, "The candidate is not admitted."

"May I ask the chairman how many negative votes were cast?" a previously silent member inquired.

"Joe, I think you know that is against our rules. We speak only as a committee."

"Well, what I would like to know then is what is it we've done as a committee. We have earlier in this meeting voted to admit a man who was convicted by a jury of his peers of murdering his wife, and we have done so not because we disagree with the verdict but because he has served his time and we are compassionate men. And now we reject a man who has what we call a 'life-style' but has been completely vindicated after facing trumped-up charges of immorality. What kind of message are we trying to send to the Alumni about qualifications for club membership?"

Brian Kennedy quickly reverted to his role as committee jester. "I think that the message is quite clear. If a University man is coming out of the club locker room and suddenly feels something pointed at his back, he wants to be sure that it's a gun."

In the darkness of the club grillroom he searched for landmarks that would guide him. It wouldn't be wise to show a light. Within a few moments his eyes had adjusted to the night, and what had been indistinct began to assume familiar shapes. Along the wall to his left, three severed heads loomed up. He could reach them if he wished without extending his arm to its full length. But there was no need to do so, he remembered the order—wildebeest, warthog, and puma. Once past them, a left turn through a wide archway would take him into the cocktail lounge.

As soon as he was in the lounge he felt safer from chance observation. He ran a finger of his free hand along the nickel rail of the bar until he found the gap between the end of the bar counter and the wall partition that separated the lounge from a game room. He quickly stepped inside the bar and flashed his penlight under the counter. There it was, dangling from a hook to which he had often seen the steward return it, the key to the wine cellar.

He unlocked the cellar door at the rear of the lounge, and made his way down slowly, preferring the dim glow of the penlight to the fluorescent ceiling fixtures that might shine up at pedestrians passing by on the street. It was cool down here, a welcome relief from the summer stuffiness that the public rooms of the club retained even in the early hours.

When he reached the bottom of the stairs, he did not take long to find what he was looking for. The bottles were stored in bins built into the walls and in rows of free-standing cabinets that divided the cellar floor into a number of aisles, as in the stacks of the University's famous library. The bins were prominently labeled by wine-growing regions—Côte de Beaune, Médoc, St. Emilion, Loire, Rhône, and Rioja. But he passed by them with little notice.

On he walked down the central aisle, which was wider than the others. He crouched in instinctive caution, because he was approaching the front building wall and could see the faint illumination of the streetlights that trickled through a high barred window directly ahead. He was still several feet from the wall when he reached his goal. The large, squat bottles of whites and reds stood upright on low tables that had been placed in the middle of the floor.

He set down the black briefcase he had been carrying in his left hand, and shone the penlight on his watch. Twelve-thirty. He went to work quickly. It was no trouble at all to unscrew the bottles and place the caps neatly at their side. He then opened the briefcase and withdrew three Mason jars which he arrayed along the edge of the nearest table. In the weak halo cast by the penlight he could see the white powder shining. He uncapped the jars and, in a few tours around the tables, funneled their contents into the wine bottles. He did not trouble to stir the wine because his experiments at home had shown that the stuff would readily dissolve.

In fact, it was really no harder than dumping chlorine into a swimming pool. Except that he must find his way back upstairs without being seen.

* * *

Paul Prye looked with disgust at the leaky pen that was the best the International Hotel could provide. Wiping his fingers, he mentally bequeathed the ballpoints to his least favorite diplomats who might occupy his room during the next session of the United Nations. Paul was an urban history professor at Columbia, but when his disapproving colleagues weren't watching too closely, he surrendered to his genuine vocation for the study and solution of true crimes, past and present. His father had celebrated Paul's double life in a small papier-mâché figurine he had commissioned when his son was awarded tenure at the university. The sculpture pictured Paul at his chaotic desk set in a corner of diplomaed walls, learned treatises at his elbow and a lecture draft before him; in his hands he lovingly cradled a dog-eared volume titled *Lizzie Borden*.

Why had the mild-mannered Paul developed a passion for crime? Perhaps it was his parents' fault. It was they who had bestowed on him the long head and aquiline profile that resembled the magazine illustrators' notion of Sherlock Holmes. And then there was the eternal embarrassment of his name. His parents, sophisticated as they were in most respects, were blithely unaware that "Paul Pry" was the inquisitive title character in an 1825 English comedy by John Poole, and that his name had become synonymous in England with "busybody." Londoners who did not simply turn from Paul in disgust when he was introduced invariably trotted out the same tiresome joke after they learned of his hobby: it was small wonder that a man so named was forever trying to uncover the real identity of Jack the Ripper. Laurence Sterne was right, Paul's learned art historian wife, Alice, liked to remark, many a promising infant has been "Nicodemused into nothingness."

Alice had for many years merely tolerated with ironic detachment her husband's preoccupation with true crimes— his ever-growing collection of trial pamphlets and *Police Gazettes*, and his little lectures on bloody deeds to literary and history clubs—for to her, fact was a poor substitute for the dizzying plots of her beloved Agatha Christie. Still, a recent trip to England had persuaded her that there was something to be said for her husband's obsession after all. In 1988, with considerable prodding on her part and with the aid of useful suggestions she had thrown out from time to time, Paul had called on his knowledge of crime history to help Scotland Yard solve the "Jack the Ripper Walking Tour Murder."

That triumph had receded for the moment from Paul's mind as he reflected bitterly on the events that had brought him to the International Hotel. He resumed his letter to his son Jeff at music camp:

> I suppose the good news is that the fire alarm worked. I'm not sure that's entirely to its credit because it also "works" every time we have a thunderstorm or your mother stir-fries scallops in her wok.
>
> The bad news, according to your mother, is that my library was spared. I suspect that in her heart of hearts she would have preferred to see my bookshelves in smoke and flames than to go on living with my dust and the insect scourge of bibliophiles that bears the beautiful name of silverfish.
>
> But this was not to be. Most of the devastation is on the first floor, in the kitchen where our decrepit toaster started the blaze going, and the dining room. On the second floor there is smoke damage almost everywhere, which will make this the Summer of the Painter.
>
> Speaking of painters, we were at the NYU lecture on frescoes at the time the toaster finally decided to burn something other than our whole wheat. You mother claims that I now owe my life to art and must stop making philistine comments at modern-sculpture shows in SoHo.
>
> If we're lucky, we'll be back home in Riverdale by the beginning of August. Meantime, as you can see from the stationery and my inky fingerprints, we're staying at the International Hotel. Tomorrow we move to the Alumni Club for the balance of our exile. It's really sort of strange how it came about. I was invited by Rodney

Baker, a big enchilada at the club. He hardly knows me at all, but he must know I am not a graduate of his august University. I really should be flattered—that is, unless he turns out to be a secret admirer of your mother.

It may all prove to be a blessing in disguise. In the conducive atmosphere of a great Stanford White building (you remember White, he was murdered by Harry Thaw in *Ragtime*), I may finally be able to buckle down to work on my long-delayed social history of the clubs and clubmen of London and New York. My files also survived the toaster's revenge. One of the private joys of publishing my club book is that it will drive my urban-studies colleagues absolutely frantic. There will be no demographics and no charts, just people, but after all, those are the creatures who, for better and often for worse, build and inhabit cities. At our last departmental meeting Professor Norton said to me, "The trouble with you, Prye, is that you fritter away your time writing what the French call *little history*." So be it, but I would love to make some progress this summer on my "little history" of urban clubs.

At least I hope I'll get some work done. Otherwise, I don't know what I'll do to stay awake during weeks of enforced lodging at the Alumni Club of New York.

Love to you and the cello.

Dad

CHAPTER I

Alice Prye stepped out of the cab, dressed in her safari outfit. It was a costume, she noted with regret, that was nowadays more commonly seen in midtown, with its khaki cotton-twill bush jacket and matching trousers. To these fundamentals Alice had added her own distinctive touch, a straw fedora over a zebra-striped scarf that hid her fine dark hair from the wind. When more conservative dressers would ask why she had omitted a pith helmet, she would say that you couldn't carry these fashion themes too far.

As he struggled with their suitcases, Paul Prye noticed a little disheveled, red-nosed man who seemed to be loitering under the canopy of the club's entrance, perhaps fearing a summer rain shower. First to Paul's surprise and then his delight, the man came forward and took the baggage; he was the club's unpretentious doorman.

At the reception desk the Pryes were greeted (if that word is bent to the breaking point) by a preoccupied young woman whose mouth was set in an emphatic downcurve that either was permanent by now or had been inspired by the entry of her new guests.

"We're the Pryes," Paul began affably. "We will be staying at least until the end of July, at the invitation of your member Rodney Baker."

The receptionist nodded unceremoniously. "Yes, I know; he's left you a note." She handed Paul an envelope.

"We'd like a nice room," Alice specified, "since we're staying so long."

"All our rooms are nice, but the seventh floor has been recently renovated."

"How close is that to the squash courts?" Alice asked suspiciously.

"They're a floor above, but our previous guests have never complained about noise."

Alice and the receptionist exchanged expressive glances. They agreed that they did not like each other.

Paul tried to referee. "We'll try a seventh-floor room."

"Do you prefer a room with double bed or twins?"

Alice shifted the issue in an unromantic direction. "Which room is larger?"

"The one with twins."

"Then we'd prefer that one—if it has lots of closet space."

Paul was puzzled. "Why do we need a lot of closet space? We haven't brought too much of our clothes with us."

"That's true," said Alice agreeably, "but I like to leave room for expansion."

Room 759 it would be. Paul signed the register, and the doorman (who represented a large fraction of the club staff) moved off with their bags. As they turned from the desk to follow him, the receptionist called Paul back. "Mr. Prye, I should mention our dress code. Gentlemen wear ties in all public areas of the club. I'd better give you a copy of our rule book."

Paul put out his right hand to accept the little oxblood volume, while with his left he clutched apologetically at his open shirt collar. Before he could mumble his excuses, further conversation was interrupted by the appearance of a middle-aged jogger, attired in sweat shirt, running shorts, and Adidas, who loped through the lobby and exited through a small street door at the side of the reception desk.

"That's the jogger's door," the receptionist explained lamely.

"So we observe," Alice replied, and turning to Paul she added in her best stage whisper, "The dress code has been amended, I see. You've got to wear a tie if you're standing still."

The Pryes left the lobby and took the corridor that led through the grillroom to the elevators. Along the wall to their left was a row of wild animal heads. A black panther appeared to stare down at safari-clad Alice with a sense of *déjà vu*.

The Pryes overtook the doorman-porter at the threshold of their room. If it had been renovated, as the receptionist claimed, the predominant influence on the interior decorator had been early-twentieth-century dormitory. The carpet sported the University's colors and the walls were off-white with tan stripes. The twin beds for which Alice had opted were wedged into the two far corners of the room. They were a far cry from the queen-size beds of the International Hotel, in fact, more like coffin-size. The rest of the furniture consisted of a bureau with warped drawers, a small night table between the beds, and a maroon-and-white wingchair that was at war with the wallpaper. After the doorman explained why the television didn't work, Paul tipped him and he left. Alice busied herself with unpacking and staking her claim to much of the closet, while Paul examined the room's crowning glory: the school photographs on the wall. The room was dedicated to the class of 1916 and the wall display gave the place of honor to three panoramic photographs of class reunions on the turf of the University's football stadium. Circling the room, Paul also examined studio portraits of the class's most distinguished members: a novelist of the Jazz Age, an architect, and a New York State politician. Some of the class members were pictured receiving decorations for gallantry in the First World War, and yellowing menus recalled annual class dinners in the postwar years. What held Paul's attention longest were action photo-

graphs of the sports victories of the class. Hopelessly unco-
ordinated, Paul had proved the ultimate challenge to the
athletic director of his own prep school. Since it was an
article of faith that all the boys had to do something for the
honor of the school's sports program, Paul was finally set to
work weeding the tennis courts. He had compensated over
the years for his lack of athletic prowess by mastering the
history and statistics of American sports with the same
passion for detail that he brought to his study of crime.

Now he was basking in the glories of the teams of 1916.
He silently cheered the University's undefeated crew, which
the photographer had frozen in the moment of its boat-
length victory over Harvard on the Charles River. To the
right was a group portrait of a formidable football team of
the same year, all smug smiles. Beneath the crew photograph
was a small photo of a running back breaking into the clear.
He bent down to read the legend: "Charlie Benson of the
University's 1916 team running for a touchdown in the 6–0
victory over Yale."

Alice called to Paul from the closet, which was rapidly
becoming her realm: "You've got all July to look at the sports
photos. Why don't you at least unpack your suits?" Receiving no answer, she went to see what he was doing and found
him feeling the wallpaper over one of the beds.

"If you're going to tell me we have rats in the walls, please
get me a drink first."

Paul turned around. "Nothing half so exciting, I'm afraid.
I had just noticed that, though this room has supposedly been
freshly decorated, some of the pictures seem to have been
removed."

Alice looked at the rear wall. On the left, arranged
vertically, were a photographic portrait and a dinner menu,
and above the night table hung the group of sports snapshots
Paul had been admiring. But over the right bed there was
nothing.

"Perhaps the decorator was Japanese," said Alice, "and
thought it was time to introduce the class of 1916 to the
beauty of asymmetry."

"No, I don't think so, because I've just located three holes that were made by picture hooks."

"We'll take care of that when we get home. I'll send them a few of our wedding pictures, assuming, of course, that they'll accept something a little more modern than 1916. But let's not worry about that now. I think I can still salvage something of the afternoon."

"What did you have in mind?" Paul asked abstractedly as he opened the note the receptionist had given him.

"If it's the hour for baring my soul, I thought I'd just have time to nip over to Thirty-eighth Street to hunt for sparkling shoulder straps. I've got a drop-dead evening gown in mind for the opera gala."

Like the lost mother in A. A. Milne's poem, Alice always thought that she could get right down to the end of town and be back in time for tea.

"You can't do that. Rodney Baker is meeting us in the club library at four-thirty."

Suspicious of a plot against her dress designing, Alice stepped behind him and read the note over his shoulder. "I don't see any mention of me at all. He probably wants to talk about fine bindings, and you Lambs know how little we women are interested in such things."

The barb was painful and well directed. The "Lambs" (whom Alice, in her more sardonic moments, referred to as the "Baa-baas") were the members of Paul's all-male book club, The Charles Lamb Society. Recently, one of the society's officers, in a newspaper interview about its admission policy, had explained that he had never met a woman who knew anything about bookbinding.

"You can't desert me," Paul insisted. "He's not going to talk about books; you can be sure of that. I don't think he's exactly a candidate for the Lambs. In fact, Alice, this note hardly comes as a surprise."

"Why do you say that?"

"Haven't you wondered why we were invited to stay here? Neither of us is a graduate of the University and we haven't taught there."

Alice offered a correction. "You've forgotten my guest lecture in 1983 on Géricault's drawings."

"So I have, but brilliant as it was, I hardly think it translates into a month's stay at the Alumni Club, particularly when arranged by an invitation couched in ambiguous terms suggesting we may not be billed for the room."

"I'm also offended that you underrate my charm."

"I'd be the last man in the world to do so," Paul said as he ushered her out of the room, "but this note smacks of quid pro quo."

Paul Prye had trouble matching names and faces. When he attended planning sessions for history symposia, he would draw the conference table at the top of the first page of his memo pad, showing the name of each of his colleagues and where they were sitting. To guard against the possibility that they might change places after a coffee break, he usually noted short descriptions after each name: "owlish," "a younger version of Alice's uncle Jim," or "like Richard Nixon with a better razor."

Rodney Baker, though, had never presented much of a problem for Paul. He had a craggy, bloodless face and, though his hair was more salt than pepper, had never seen any reason to change the crew cut he had undoubtedly favored three decades before when he was at the University. But what made him memorable even to Paul was his posture. When he talked in his curious halting style he hooked a thumb in his belt and struck an angular pose, putting his weight on one leg and jutting out the opposite hip and elbow; he writhed slightly as if urging on his words. It was an attitude that must have been copied from somewhere, Paul had often thought, without being able to pin down the source. Today, as Baker met the Pryes at the library door and immediately took his familiar stance, Paul wondered whether Rodney was unconsciously recreating some favorite characters from the movies, a strange blend of gunslingers and the Elephant Man.

The Pryes had met him many years before, but never managed to get to know him well. Rodney had sold his inherited business two decades ago and become the perennial mayor of his suburb. He was active in a number of major cultural organizations including the Philharmonic, and it was at a fund-raiser for the orchestra that the Pryes had first been introduced to him. His political experience and board service had taught him to guard his words, or perhaps his penchant for secrecy was inborn. Alice, who lived in hope for the inside story, referred to him as the "trustee type."

"Welcome to the club," Baker said to the Pryes, drawing on his limited stores of cordiality. "I hope you'll enjoy your stay, though I regret the circumstances that bring you here. How are the repairs going?"

"We settled with the insurance company today," Alice replied, "and the work will begin next week."

"That's wonderful," said Baker absently, as he led the Pryes into a meeting room that adjoined the library and closed the door. At the far end of a very long, oak boardroom table ornately carved in a style Alice called "early Inquisition" sat a fat little gray-haired man in a rumpled navy poplin suit. "Paul and Alice," Rodney said, "meet Vic Baines, the perennial chairman of our House Committee."

"Is your room satisfactory?" Baines asked as he filled his pipe, a leather-encased meerschaum similar to Paul's favorite before he surrendered his smoking habit to Alice's allergies.

"Excellent," Paul said, blotting out his memory of the beds, and Alice added, "Great closet."

Baker drew back chairs for the Pryes beside Baines but remained standing, thumb grasping his belt, as he said,

"I'm sure you know the place pretty well from your past visits here and that you'll feel right at home. And one detail I should mention. Please sign all your charges with my audit number, BA-114."

"How will we arrange to reimburse you?" Paul asked.

"Paul, you embarrass me. I thought I'd made it clear that you are here as my guests or, perhaps I should say, as guests of the club." He looked in Baines' direction for a sign of concurrence, but none appeared as the house chairman smoked on.

"We can't let you do that," Paul objected. "Alice and I aren't even graduates."

"We would love to be able to claim the Pryes, but the University's loss was Harvard's gain." Rodney accompanied his compliment with a fleeting smile and then lapsed into a long silence. When the Pryes were beginning to wonder whether the welcoming ceremony had ended, Baker said, "Paul, there is a small favor you could do for us while you're here."

Paul flashed a knowing glance to Alice. Here it comes. The price of the visit. A sudden worry struck him, a worry that had been fostered by the unheralded presence of Vic Baines. Paul had a bad habit of talking about his scholarly projects long before they made their way from his notebooks to the word processor. He knew he had been guilty of boring many friends and dinner companions about his research on gentlemen's clubs. Perhaps Baker and Baines were about to commission a brief history of the Alumni Club for the price of a month's free rent. If so, it was back to the International Hotel, leaky pens and all.

"How do you think I could help you gentlemen?" Paul asked with as noncommittal a tone as he could convey.

"Do you remember the pleasant party at the Stanhopes' last spring?" Baker asked. "You were in superb form that night and were immensely entertaining with your stories about your crime researches."

"It was probably Phyllis Stanhope who got him started," Alice said spitefully. "She's one of Paul's true-crime groupies. She loves him for the dangers other people have passed."

Paul pretended to ignore her. "I do recall the evening and I hope I didn't run on too much. It seems to me I drank quite a lot of champagne. In any event, I don't see how my amateur criminology could be of the slightest use to you. I am assuming, of course, that all our fellow guests at the Stanhopes' arrived home safe and sound."

Rodney did not smile and Vic Baines was expressionless as

he continued to puff on his meerschaum. "I'm afraid they're not the group I am worried about," Baker replied. "Let me ask you this: What do you know about threatening letters?"

Before Paul could answer, Alice intervened. "Before you let him start, you would be wise to take a leaf from Phyllis Stanhope's book and order in a *catered* dinner. We'll be nothing but bleached bones by the time he finishes his lecture."

As if to confirm Alice's pessimistic forecast, Paul said; "As a matter of fact, threatening letters, and anonymous letters generally, are a favorite subject of mine and a very complicated one."

He brought himself up short. Here he was beginning to act like a medical specialist, warming with enthusiasm for a rare disease without stopping to consider whether the men with whom he spoke might be suffering from the malady. "How is it that you have developed an interest in threatening letters?"

Rodney took a long club envelope from his breast pocket and broke the seal. He removed three Xeroxed letter-sized pages and spread them on the table before the Pryes.

Paul rearranged the letters in chronological order from left to right and he and Alice read them together, nodding to each other to confirm that they had finished one and were ready to move on to the next. The first letter was dated in April.

Dear Ms. Scroop,

I hasten to express my sorrow at the sudden passing of an Alumni Club stalwart and your "good friend," Miles Corbett.

Yours was truly a beautiful relationship and one that those of us who knew you both are sorry to see cut off in its bloom. You had proved to us all that with the divorce rate nearing 50 percent, there is a lot to be said for the special kind of unwedded bliss you shared with Miles, based on love and not on fidelity.

Miles was, of course, the greatest drama critic who ever graced the pages of the *Town Tonsil*. Many members had the pleasure of watching him perfect his slashing style as an undergraduate reviewer for the *Oxblood*, and his career in New York has, if anything, exceeded their wildest hopes.

We must face the inevitable fact (and I'm sure you do) that a critic's life is not a happy one. Miles was no exception. His ears must often have burned with the tale that he never stayed until the final curtain and was generally to be found at Sardi's bar during the third act. But what else could a man as literate as Miles do in this sad era of the theater's decline? He had no choice but to drown his sorrows over the thinness and predictability of today's Broadway fare.

In any event, it seems to me that Miles's drinking problem has been grossly exaggerated, and that the cause of his death, when confirmed, will not be alcoholism.

Respectfully yours,

A Friend from the Alumni Club

The next letter, considerably shorter, was dated in early June:

Dear Ms. Morrison,

Please accept my sincere condolences in the death of Vance Parry, your company's beloved CEO and a favorite here at the Alumni Club.

Vance will be remembered by his friends and the general business community as a man who always followed the dictates of his own judgment, regardless of public opinion. When he nominated you to the board of directors there were those know-it-alls who smiled and whispered, but Vance knew you were the best-qualified candidate. Who can say he was wrong?

In closing, if you will permit a comment that may be out of place on this sad occasion, I would like to congratulate you on your company's successful bankruptcy reorganization under Chapter 11.

In shared grief,

A Friend from the Alumni Club

The final letter was addressed to Mrs. Richardson and expressed sympathy for the death of her husband, John. It was dated July 7. Casting his mind back, Paul recalled that it was on July 9 that he received a telephone call from Rodney Baker inviting them to stay at the Alumni Club.

When they had read the last letter, Paul rocked his head quizzically. "What makes you call these threatening letters? They look to me like sarcastic condolence notes written by someone who wasn't all that fond of the dear departed."

"Suppose we were to add the fact that none of the 'dear departed' is dead. In fact, all of them are alive and well and highly respected members of this club."

"Then I would have to conclude that these letters are, to put it mildly, in the worst possible taste."

Between drafts on his pipe Vic Baines offered his first contribution to the dialogue. "Isn't it possible, though, that the letter writer wishes these men dead and might be warning them that some day soon genuine condolence notes will be in order?"

"That would be a pretty big leap for me to make," Paul answered. "I'd have to know a lot more than I can gather from a quick reading of these letters. Can you tell us something about the men our letter writer has prematurely buried?"

Baker looked at Baines, who nodded that Rodney should proceed. "In an odd, distorted way, the key facts are there in the letters. Miles Corbett is the lead theater critic of the *Town Tonsil*. Do you know his work?"

"We don't read the *Tonsil*. I may have seen quotes from his reviews from time to time in Broadway ads. Have you ever read him, Alice?"

"I don't think so, but he was once a guest on "Entertainment Tonight." He didn't seem to like much of anything."

"That's not surprising," Vic Baines interjected. "He's not the most generous of the town's reviewers, but as far as I know there is no basis for the letter writer's claim that he docsn't sit through thc plays hc reviews."

"What about the drinking?" Alice asked.

"He likes his cocktails, but he's never been any problem here at the club. At least nobody's complained to the House Committee."

"I think we've heard of Vance Parry," said Alice, who was beginning to find the theme of the meeting more promising than she would have predicted. "Isn't he the chief executive at Parry Enterprises who got all the bad press for promoting his girlfriend to the board?" Although Paul and Alice were both children of stockbrokers, business stories were more her cup of tea, particularly when aromatic with scandal.

Baker nodded as he finally took a seat at Alice's left. "You're right, it's the same Parry. The truth of the matter is that Marian Morrison's spectacular rise at the company had nothing to do with their personal relationship. When Parry is at the office he forgets that anyone has a private life, himself included, and he was astounded that anyone could think that Marian's success was based on anything but merit. The aftermath, of course, was sad. It was shortly after the nasty gossip about Marian began that Parry Enterprises' operations went into a steep decline, resulting in its bankruptcy filing two years ago. I think the reason was that Vance no longer could keep his mind on his work. His romance with Marian had not distracted him in the slightest, but even his powers of concentration could not resist the daily press barrage that followed her board appointment."

"Is it true that Parry Enterprises is out of Chapter 11? I don't remember reading that." Alice was a daily reader of the *Wall Street Journal*, which she turned to right after *Women's Wear Daily*.

"The letter writer was taking liberties there," Rodney answered, "though Vance tells me that he's close to agreement with creditors."

"I think we both know who Richardson is," Paul said. "Isn't he the fellow who served under Nixon and Ford in the Treasury Department?"

"Yes," Baines confirmed in an almost pedantic manner, "his brush with disaster in the Watergate proceedings was a close one, but those of us who know him well are convinced that the charges against him were politically motivated. There had been talk at the time of his running for Governor or the Senate."

"Are all three men active at the club?" Paul asked as he looked again at the Richardson letter.

Baines looked at the ceiling as smoke rings ascended from his pipe. His answer was measured and judicious. "Corbett and Richardson have been extremely active. As you see from the Richardson letter, he was a president of the club. I wouldn't say that Vance Parry was terribly active, because he has very little time for any nonbusiness matters, but I should add parenthetically that he has been very generous in gifts to the club's endowment campaigns."

"Are these the only letters that have been received from the"—Paul squinted at the close of the Richardson letter— "Friend from the Alumni Club?"

Rodney Baker shrugged. "We really don't know. There may be others who have received letters but kept it to themselves. But the people who've received the letters we've shown you are hopping mad about it and particularly resent the fact that these letters are coming from the club."

"You really don't know that," Paul said cautiously. "What we know is that they are written on club stationery and signed anonymously 'a Friend from the Alumni Club.' Do I assume correctly that this stationery would be available at writing desks in the public areas of the club?"

"Yes. There are desks in the lobby, in the Great Hall, and on the gallery outside the library."

Paul continued. "So it would be easy for a nonmember, who was not as fortunate as we in being given lodging privileges, to have obtained the club stationery. It should be noted further that the anonymous letter writer does not explicitly state that he is a club member. He signs merely as 'a friend.'"

"I'm not sure I agree with you there," said Alice. "Doesn't the Richardson letter indicate pretty clearly that the signatory is a club member?"

Paul made a half-concession. "He certainly poses there as an insider who knows club politics. But note his peculiar phrasing, for example: 'I, and all the members of the Alumni Club, sympathize with you in John's untimely death.' He does not say, 'I and all the other members.' But you may be right in suggesting that I am making too much of this point because if the 'Friend' indeed purports to be a club member, I am not sure that an anonymous letter writer has a high degree of credibility even as to his own identity. I would still have to say that at the moment we must recognize the possibility that the stationery was filched by an outsider from the public areas of the club and written and posted at his leisure from some other location. In any event, it isn't likely that a stranger would have written all these letters on the club premises and risked being discovered in the throes of composition."

Rodney shook his head. "You're partly wrong, I'm afraid. We know that the letters were mailed from the club."

"How is that?"

Rodney seemed embarrassed. "I didn't think of bringing you Xerox copies of the envelopes, but I'll correct that error tomorrow. We have a habit at the club of stamping outgoing mail with reminders of upcoming events. It's my recollection, for example, that the Richardson envelope carried a reminder of tomorrow night's New Members' Party. We really carry this practice to ridiculous extremes, and I know Vic Baines and his House Committee don't approve at all. We've had suppliers turn out in force for films of the Harvard game because the stamped reminders had appeared that month on our accounts-payable envelopes.

"In any event," Baines said, ignoring the reference to his committee, "our members are not taking kindly to receiving fictitious death notices on the club letterhead. They want the mailings to stop."

"Has anyone thought of going to the police?" Paul asked.

While Vic Baines tapped his pipe on a club ashtray, Baker answered. "There's been some talk of it, but nobody's

willing to take that step yet. The Alumni Club dreads
publicity. There is some concern that the letters contain
veiled death threats, but it is possible that your first reaction
was in fact correct, that all we have here is a malicious joke.
Nobody wants to look foolish to the police, and least of all
do we want to run the risk of an overreaction that would
encourage the letter writer to expand his campaign. So what
we were hoping was that, while you are here, you might be
able to put some of your crime know-how to work by
conducting a low-key investigation."

Paul was tempted by the proposal though he was chas-
tened by the knowledge that embarking on a poison-pen-
letter investigation was not the best way to advance his work
on his club history. While he pondered his response, Alice
came to his aid. "I am sure that Paul is going to mull for a few
moments so that he can hide the exuberance with which he
will then accept your request. Am I right, Paul? But just to
make the project clearer, may I ask, Rodney, whether you
two are making this suggestion on your own or in behalf of
the club administration?"

It was now Rodney's turn to pause. "Let me say that
Vic Baines and I have strongly urged that we approach Paul
for help and that the club administration will facilitate
his efforts. Whatever we can do to help, you have only to
ask."

Paul took him at his word. "The first thing you could do
for me would be to arrange for me to see Corbett, Parry, and
Richardson, that is, if they'll see me."

"I think they will if we ask."

"I also ought to see the club president."

Baker writhed in silence for a moment, in laborious search
of the right words, and Vic Baines did not come to his
assistance. "In the normal course of events you would be
right, that would be the appropriate beginning. But I'm
afraid it's not going to be possible. Jim Preswick spends all
summer at the Vineyard."

Paul adjusted quickly to this temporary setback. "It would

also be extremely helpful if I could have a current roster of the club's officers and committees."

"No problem at all. You'll find that in the club rule book, which is available at reception."

"He's already been given a copy of that," Alice said wryly. "He made the mistake of entering the lobby half-dressed."

"Half-dressed?" Baines repeated.

"Yes, open collar but no Adidas."

"I see what you mean. I hope that our Miss Gustave didn't give you too hard a time. If she did, the House Committee will be cross with her because we do want your stay to get off to a pleasant start."

"And to help celebrate your arrival," Rodney Baker added, "I would like you both to be my guests at the cocktail party we're giving here tomorrow evening in honor of the new members. I hope you can join us."

"We'd be delighted," Paul said vaguely, his mind still on the letters that lay before him. "Can I take these?"

"Of course you can. We brought them for you," Rodney said, folding the letters and reinserting them in the envelope, which he then handed to Paul.

Paul thanked him and added, "These will get me started, but I'll eventually need the originals."

Nodding agreement, Rodney replied, "No problem. I think you can count on having them." He then qualified his words. "At least some of them."

As Rodney was about to escort the Pryes into the library, Paul stopped him for a final word. "Rodney, before we say good-bye, I will be brave and raise the question that we've been too polite to ask. Has either of you received one of these letters?"

An unaccustomed hint of pink came to Rodney's cheeks. "Of course not. Do you think we'd show you these awful notes that others have had the guts to bring in and hide our own at home?"

Vic Baines added, "That's right, and speaking for myself, I should say parenthetically that I just wouldn't fit the pattern of the letters. My wife Laura died five years ago, and the Friend would have nobody to condole with on my death."

"It was a foolish question," Paul said. "I'm sorry that I asked."

But Paul was not sure that he could believe either of them. As Alice would put it, each was the "trustee type."

CHAPTER 2

On the way back to their room, the Pryes took a detour to the cocktail lounge. Alice ordered a Swedish vodka, and Paul asked for a double Scotch, which he found, as Dr. Johnson had said of the prospects of being hanged, concentrated the mind wonderfully.

"Paul, it may have escaped your attention, but you have become a very unresponsive man." As she spoke, Alice admired the crystal purity of the vodka with her art historian's eye.

"How is that?" asked Paul, somewhat disconcerted by her unexpected comment. "I have no idea what you are talking about. Have I been sitting here ignoring you?"

"You know that isn't the problem. I wouldn't tolerate being ignored for a minute. It's Rodney Baker who's entitled to be angry with you for successfully dodging his first question."

Paul couldn't remember. "And what was that?"

"He began our odd little conference by asking 'What do you know about threatening letters?' but you kept him and Vic Baines so busy answering your questions that you never told him. So now you can make up for your bad manners by

telling me succinctly everything I should know about threatening letters. Why in the world do people send them?"

With an unconvincing grimace of reluctance, Paul threw
himself into the subject. "For as many reasons as any deviant
conduct. The most straightforward is extortion. In fact,
around the turn of the century the so-called Blackhanders
(thugs drawn from the Neapolitan Camorra mobs and their
Mafia rivals) made a regular racket of extortion letters
warning people to pay up or die. But the extortionist is not
always looking for money. He may be trying to induce his
victim to do something he wants done (like marrying him) or
to stop the victim from doing something he doesn't want
done (like marrying someone else)."

"In principle then, if you do what the extortionist wants
you to do, he should stop writing."

Paul agreed in part. "That is if he is a logical extortionist
and easily satisfied."

"All right," Alice said impatiently. "I accept the possibility
that there may not be honor among blackmailers—or what
do you call them, Blackhanders?—but let's put them aside. If
the letters Rodney and Baines gave you meant to contain
veiled threats, I don't see any hint how one is supposed to go
about making the writer happy. Are some threateners quite
implacable? In other words, do they simply tell you what
harm they'll do and then perform as promised?"

Paul nodded. "Quite commonly that's precisely what
happens. The threat is a show of power and an attempt to
heighten the terror of the victim by forcing him to anticipate
the criminal's blow. It's the hardest kind of threat to deal with
because there is no way to ward it off except by capturing the
letter writer or putting his target under uncomfortably close
guard. And just as in the present case, the trick is to
distinguish between a crank letter and a genuine murder
plot."

"I don't see the hand of the mob in the Alumni Club
letters, do you?" asked Alice. "Suppose we're dealing instead
with some kind of private threat. Should we worry that in

most cases of that kind, the writer's going to attempt some mischief?"

"It's hard to say," Paul answered. "In many circumstances the threat leads nowhere. The obvious example is the crank letter. Assuming the crank has some notion at least of what he's doing, his intention may be no more than to strike terror or cause confusion. When the writer has some personal grievance against his target, the letter itself may be the strongest act of violence of which he's capable and he may realize that from the very beginning. In some cases, though, he may be testing his own capacity for violence, sending his letters as a first step—perhaps then devising more drastic means of disrupting his enemy's life, but satisfying his enmity at some point short of physical attack.

"I'm not sure, though, that these Alumni Club letters were intended to threaten anyone." He handed the letters to her across the cocktail table. "I would be glad to have your interpretation."

Alice opened the envelope and spread the letters out on the table. "As you know, I will hold in these matters, as in all crime puzzles, with the divine principles of Agatha Christie. She and all her imitators have taught us that death threats are meaningless; that the murderer turns them out wholesale to distract the attention of the police—and the reader—while he is busily embarked on a completely unrelated murder plot."

Paul frowned in mock earnestness. "So that, according to Agatha Christie's teachings, our letter writer is threatening members of the Alumni Club as a cover for an intended attack at an American Legion post."

"Something like that," Alice said leniently, as if encouraging one of the better pupils in a slow reading group. "What do you think of this phrase, for example?"

As she was about to impress him with her literary analysis, she felt a polite tap on her shoulder. It was one of the waiters. In silence he pointed to a card in the wire menu holder in the middle of their table. As Paul and Alice scanned the card, they realized that they had violated still another house rule:

Unless the House Committee gives special written permission in advance (which it is unlikely to do under most circumstances), members shall not display in public areas of the club any papers that seem to have a business character.

Politely acknowledging the rebuke, Paul signed his check and they left the lounge. On their way out, Alice muttered, "Darling, you really are getting to be a pushover. We had him on a technicality, I don't think insulting condolence notes have a 'business character.'"

When they arrived at the door of their room, Alice began to wonder whether Paul's Scotch had been perilously close to a triple. He seemed to be taking an ungodly amount of time fumbling at the lock. If she had looked more closely, though, she would have seen that he was running his right hand across a portion of the door panel above the lock. He could feel under his fingertips a distinct quadrangular ridge under the fresh coat of varnish.

The Pryes decided to have dinner at the club that night; the next day was Saturday and Alice had planned a full itinerary that would lead her from an early-morning Chelsea flea market to the galleries of Madison Avenue. After his shower, Paul shaved with almost microscopic attention, fearing a sternly worded house rule against five-o'clock shadow. Alice was launching a new wrap and tied silk jersey skirt and was having roughly equal amounts of trouble with the wrapping and tying.

Paul was sympathetic. "You seem to be making some progress, but I don't think you'll miss me for a few minutes." If she heard him at all, she did not object, so he slipped away.

His first stop was the front lobby. It was empty except for a tired-looking young woman who sat on a worn leather couch facing the street door. Wrapped in a white fox stole as if she had heard that the balmy summer weather would abruptly end, she consulted her watch and frowned impatiently. She won't notice me at all, Paul thought. He sat down at the writing desk across from her and dashed off a short note. He pretended to return the club pen to its holder but in fact wrapped it in the note paper and sealed them both in an envelope he then casually thrust into his jacket pocket. Needless sleight of hand, the woman wasn't looking in his direction. He repeated this operation at a desk near the monumental fireplace in the Great Hall. Two pairs of chess players sat at the far end of the large smoky room but hadn't the slightest awareness of Paul's presence. Yet had they looked they might have caught him committing an offense that was considered heinous under the traditions of clubland, stealing a pen from the writing desk.

The addition to his pen collection safely stowed, Paul returned to the lobby and walked up the grand staircase. It was one of the glories of the club building and a masterful conception of Stanford White, a double marble stairway with decorative iron balustrades executed after seventeenth-century French designs. At the top of the staircase, at a height of two stories above the ground floor, a graceful colonnaded gallery in the Palladian manner allowed a promenade around the walls of the Great Hall below. Following the west gallery to the left, Paul came to a door that led into the library and nearby he found the third writing desk. Since nobody was in sight, he pocketed the pen without the caution he had taken downstairs.

His final stop was in the library, now completely deserted. He quickly located the last two annual reports of the club, and discovered, as he suspected, that the information he wanted was in the more recent volume. His next step was to consult the card catalog, which enabled him to find the sports book he needed without difficulty. It was profusely illustrated and for an Alumni publication bore a shamelessly commercial title: *Gridiron Glory: The Early History of the University's Football Team*. Restraining his curiosity for the time being, he put the hefty volume under his arm and went back to his room to claim Alice. He found her wrapped and tied to gorgeous effect, and waiting to be taken to dinner. She wasn't very angry, because he had been away less than half an hour. Life is short, but Alice's dressing, like all arts, was long.

Alice was a thieving magpie. She always left on their trips with wire hangers and returned with wooden ones emblazoned with the names of European hotels. She had appropriated so many ashtrays from favorite dining spots that Paul referred to their home as "Alice's restaurant." He claimed that she had once cast a longing eye on a soup tureen and had been deterred from stealing it from their table only because that night she had carried a small antique beaded bag.

Given her light-fingered past, Alice was impressed with Paul's successful raid on the club's pens. "What are you going to do with them?" she asked, after she had noted nothing collectible on their table in the main dining room and turned with resignation to examining the menu.

"I will begin my mission with an act of treachery. When Baker gives me the original letters I will promptly hand them over to Dave Emmerich, together with the pens, so that he can run comparative chemical tests of the ink and check any peculiarities in the impressions that might suggest one of the pens was used."

Dave Emmerich was a lieutenant in the Manhattan Detective Command. He was a great friend of Paul's, sharing his enthusiasm for New York's crime history. They spent many Sundays together touring the area's historic murder sites, the West Twenty-third Street address at which philanthropist Benjamin Nathan had been mysteriously shot, or the Hoboken locale where the original of Edgar Allan Poe's Marie Roget had been attacked and thrown into the Hudson.

"Marvelous," cheered Alice. "And I have another great idea for you from Fritz Lang's M, which I saw a few weeks ago at MOMA, when I was supposed to be at the library. What you do is find some wood fibers clinging to the letters and match them against every table surface in the building."

"I'll tell Emmerich," Paul promised with a smile. "I don't think he goes to the movies."

"Of course, I suppose that even if we can identify the desk where the notes were written, we'll still have a long way to go before we find out who wrote the damn things."

"That will be up to me," Paul said as he turned to the à la carte page, remembering that the club was paying. "Once we've zeroed in on some suspects, I'll have to find a way to round up some writing samples."

"But the notes are printed," Alice reminded him, "and in block capitals."

"That won't stop friend Emmerich if he gets the right people into the act. The Postal Service crime laboratory has had remarkable success identifying handprinting. I've only glanced briefly at the Xerox copies, and of course am far from an expert in questioned documents, but even my untutored eye can readily spot a number of quirks in the printing style. The letters slant strongly upwards from left to right and not at all gradually at that. When we got back to the room, safe from the club rules, take a look at the signature, 'A Friend from the Alumni Club.' The first two words are on the lowest plane, the next three a step higher, and the word 'Club' appears on a lonely eminence. Then, too, some of the capitals are formed oddly. For example, the sides of the *A* crisscross like the poles of a tepee."

At this point they broke off the conversation because their waiter had begun to hover. The cutoff hour for orders was beginning to approach, what the Pryes referred to as "surly service time." After more than twenty years of marriage the Pryes had formed the habit of ordering the same main course, and tonight was no exception: veal Florentine. Their tastes in appetizers also generally coincided, unless Paul hankered for pâté de foie gras, which made Alice sneeze. (She would often lament, wiping the allergic tears from her eyes, "Nobody knows the truffles I've seen.") But they tended to quarrel over the choice of wine, both as to quantity and color.

"What do you say to a bottle of Chardonnay?" Paul asked, as he hailed the wine steward.

"Absolutely not. I don't know when you will learn to stop

plying me with seas of wine; I've already agreed to marry
you. And you know I prefer red with veal, whatever your
wine books may teach. A glass of the house Algerian
nineteen eighty-yesterday will be just fine."

With regret Paul ordered a half bottle of Chardonnay from
the wine steward, who then counseled Alice on the house
reds. She ultimately accepted his recommendation of an
Italian regional, which he asserted to be a close cousin of
Barolo.

It was an excellent dinner, they agreed; the Pryes were
easily satisfied by veal in all its varieties. They were well into
their salads when Alice returned to the day's preoccupation.
"Suppose that your first reaction was right and they're not
death threats. What sort of oddball would send out anonymous insults? Understand, of course, that I reserve the right
to reject everything you may say because Dame Agatha has
instructed me to regard these missives as smoke screens."

"It's too early to say she would be wrong," Paul answered,
"but you'll forgive me if I prefer to rely on my master
Locard." Edmond Locard, sometimes called the Sherlock
Holmes of France, had presided over the forensic laboratory
at Lyons. He had written voluminously on anonymous
letters, as on virtually every other province of crime and
detection; most of a shelf in Paul's library was devoted to his
works.

"Locard, after a long career of dealing with these unlovely
communications has, I think, drawn a very useful personality
portrait of the poison-pen addict: he generally shows a lack of
courage that may be accompanied by a joy in striking a blow
without running the risk of discovery."

"But why does he strike the blow at all?" asked Alice,
unconvinced as always by broad generalization.

"For the same motives that would cause more courageous
men to attack more directly. What does Wilde say about
murder? The coward does it with a word and the brave man
with a sword."

"I think you've twisted his meaning a little bit," caviled
Alice, "but I'll let it pass."

Paul overlooked her critique. "So we can find behind the poison-pen letter all the motives associated with violent crime: the vengeance of the discharged servant, the anger of the rejected or frustrated lover. Or the purpose of the writer may be at once more rational and less weighty so that, for example, we may find a landlord slipping insulting letters under the door of the tenant whom he wants to induce to leave so that he can jack up the rent.

"The trouble is, though, that much anonymous letter writing seems to be a pathological syndrome with no identifiable motivation at all. The French psychiatrists refer to it as 'graphorrhea,' literally, lack of pen control. The disease is marked by a number of symptoms. I've already mentioned the weakness of motives; another is the sheer volume of the correspondence. Some people afflicted with graphorrhea have been known to send as many as two or three hundred letters to one or more victims, and once there is a virulent breakout of the disorder, the copycat syndrome may be touched off. Sometimes members of an entire family collaborate on the correspondence, and in fact epidemics of anonymous letter writing have been detected in certain communities.

"Finally, the truly compulsive wielder of the poison pen tends to follow certain behavior patterns in confronting his own activity. In the first place he virtually never confesses even if he is caught in the act with the ink still on his fingers. And even more strangely, he often addresses some of the most defamatory letters to himself, not, as Agatha Christie would have it, as a 'smoke screen' but because he does not exempt himself from the hatred he has for others."

"Bravo," Alice exclaimed as she toasted Paul with the remainder of her wine. "A concise and comprehensive summary that would have been even more admirable if it didn't show the fatal sign of your old-fashioned liberalism."

Paul seemed nonplussed, so Alice proceeded, "Isn't it a fact, my gallant professor, that most poison-pen letters are written by women?"

"I believe that is often said to be the case, but unless

carefully qualified, such a statement could be misleading. Certainly, genuine threatening letters are not a predominantly feminine activity. I never heard it suggested that the Blackhand was an equal-opportunity employer. I think that particularly in past eras of sexual repression, anonymous letters were often written by women, even respectable ones, who felt rejected by men. You'll recall the case of La Roncière cited in *The French Lieutenant's Woman*. Locard refers to such letters as a sort of psychological equivalent of sexuality. I'm not clear that we see this phenomenon so often since the sexual revolution has triumphed."

Alice did not want to let him off the hook so easily. "I sometimes suspect that with the onslaught of the AIDS epidemic the sexual revolution may now have entered its days of Thermidor. Remind me, though, what was it that La Roncière's lady friend wrote?"

"The girl's name was Marie de Morell. She wrote a series of shocking letters to herself and other members of her household that she intended would be attributed to Lieutenant La Roncière.

"In the last letter she described a purely imaginary sexual assault on her by the young lieutenant. So you see that Marie's case illustrates two of the classic symptoms of graphorrhea, the use of anonymous letters as a sex surrogate, and the writer's common tendency to write the most insulting letters to himself."

Alice returned to her main objection. "Why do you continue to insist on 'himself'? Marie was a woman. Aren't there women members at the Alumni Club, and isn't it more than likely that 'A Friend from the Alumni Club' will turn out to be a female?"

Paul held up a hand to slow her onrush. "If you give me a chance, I'll answer yes to some of your questions at least. You're right that there are women members of the club, and quite a few by now if I judge rightly from a quick look at the membership roster in the rule book. The merger of the women's college with the University was completed almost a decade ago if my memory is right, but it can't be more than two years since the first woman member was admitted here. The Alumni Club doesn't move quickly."

"I should say not, since they still retain a male plural in their name. Wouldn't it be easy to rename themselves the Graduates' Club?"

Alice received the menu from the waiter and began to turn her mind to the more serious subject of dessert. When she had ordered she said to Paul, "Mark my word, you are likely to stumble if you exclude the possibility that the letter writer is a frustrated woman."

"That is a possibility," Paul acknowledged, "but I prefer to start with a different question. Who or what is the target of the letter writer's hostility?"

"What do you mean by that? Isn't that just the other side of the same question?"

"You may be right. I'll have to think about that, and if you're still game, why don't we sort things out further over breakfast? Here come our double-dark chocolate cakes."

As usual, they had ordered the same thing.

After dinner the Pryes prowled the game room in search of a *Times*; they were beginning to give thought to evening plans for the next week. Paul found a dismembered copy of the paper and reassembled it as best he could on one of the card tables. "On Wednesday," he suggested optimistically, "the City Opera's doing *Aida*."

"Any elephants?"

"I don't think there would be in a summer production."

"Then it's no go; I hate vegetarian *Aida*s," Alice ruled dismissively. "We could always spend Wednesday here, that is, if our house privileges extend to special events. I noticed on the bulletin board that it's Bessarabian Night 'with all your favorite Bessarabian dishes.' Aren't they something with an admixture of vampires? Alternatively, we could consider—" Suddenly Alice broke off in mid-sentence. The odd sensation she'd felt briefly during dessert had returned, a troubling dizziness, a constriction of the jaw and temples and a chill that clamped the nape of her neck. "Paul, would you mind if we go back to the room? I don't feel well."

"Should we call Dr. Simon?" he asked as he helped her from her chair, trying to sound calm. He was not at his best in emergencies.

"There's no need," she said, "and don't worry; I know what it is."

It was only when they returned to their room that she told him: "Chinese Restaurant Syndrome."

"At the Alumni Club?" he asked incredulously. "How could that be?" They were both allergic to monosodium glutamate, but it bothered Alice a lot more. One of the rituals of their frequent trips to Paris was a lunch at the Yellow Mountain, a Chinese restaurant on the Rue Tournon. Alice would always conclude their order with the stern injunction, "Pas de MSG," but Paul was convinced that the waiter (who was Vietnamese and didn't understand a word of French or English) hadn't the foggiest idea what she was talking about.

"Let me warn you," said Alice, who had now fully recovered (but did not ward off his neck massage), "MSG has invaded the West, borne on the wings of the killer bees."

"But I didn't have the slightest symptom," Paul protested, "and we ordered exactly the same dinner." He thought for a moment. "Except, of course, for the wine. Could it have been your wine?"

Alice smiled. "I get the point. It's my own fault. We could have had a simply enormous bottle of Chardonnay if I hadn't insisted on a glass of Italian red of doubtful pedigree. I suppose, though, it could have been worse; at least it wasn't antifreeze. Still, it's strange, isn't it, to put MSG in wine?"

"It's probably pretty bland stuff that needs a little help."

"More than a little," Alice complained, "I don't remember ever having had such an acute attack; they must have poured in great heaps of MSG. I hope it's the exporter we should blame, Paul. You don't suppose they'd do that to us at the club?"

Paul didn't answer but he opened a small spiral notebook he always kept in his inside breast pocket to record random thoughts for his lectures or writings. He penciled the words: "See Wine Committee."

When Paul came out of the bathroom, he found Alice on the bed in the far corner, reading a Manet catalog. She wore only her large black-rimmed glasses, the article of clothing she always removed with the greatest reluctance. She looked like a bespectacled odalisque.

"I do want to stress with you, Paul, that I am *completely* recovered from the MSG episode."

"I am glad for the reassurance. Whose place, yours or mine?"

"Don't be absurd, what kind of woman do you think I am? This is our first night, so it will be yours, of course. Subsequent arrangements will depend on your behavior." She transferred lithely to the other bed.

As he reached to turn off the light, Paul grumbled about the small beds that had come as a price of Alice's capacious closet. She assured him that the bed was just about right. "You know full well, Paul, how I hate queen-size. I never did fancy much going on 'search and enjoy' missions."

CHAPTER 3

The Pryes were awakened at 2 A.M. by a telephone call. It was the club engineer, who inquired apologetically whether their toilet or bathtub was overflowing; the guests in the room below had complained that their ceiling was leaking. Paul invited the engineer to take a look for himself. He arrived in a few minutes, banged at the toilet with a wrench, perhaps added a magic chant for good measure, and disappeared with another apology.

"Fire or no fire, this is the last time we stay in Room 759," Paul muttered as he thrashed about in his narrow bed.

"It could have been worse." Alice's airy voice came to him across the darkness. "They might have put us in Room 659."

An hour later the phone rang again. Paul recognized the voice of the engineer. This time there was a new crisis in the club's utilities. The engineer asked them to turn off their air conditioner. To soothe Paul's feelings, he added that he was making the same request of all the other guests; the overload on this hot summer night had caused a total power failure in the club building. It often happened in July and August, he explained.

At 8 A.M. the Pryes received a third call, this time (much to their relief) from Rodney Baker. He told them that he had arranged an appointment for Paul to call on Miles Corbett at eleven o'clock. Vance Parry had been out last night but Baker had left a message on his machine.

"With Parry's company in the shape it's in," remarked Alice on the extension, "I'm surprised you didn't get Dial-a-Prayer."

Baker forced an unconvincing giggle. "Clearly right. To be frank, Richardson's the one I'm going to have to work on hardest. He's been through a lot and is pretty mad about the letter. Oh, and about the originals. I think I can promise you at least two when I see you at the club this evening. Richardson again may be a stumbling block."

Paul thanked him and went into the bathroom to prepare Alice's traditional breakfast in bed, Wheat Thins and instant Café Hag. They should have gone downstairs for the club continental (particularly since everything went on Baker's tab), but their old touring habits were hard to break cold turkey.

Sipping regally, Alice was ready to continue her review of his investigation plans.

"When we broke off last night, I said, 'Cherchez la femme,' and you stubbornly responded, 'Pick the victim.' See if you can explain your delphic words quickly enough for me to arrive at the flea market at a respectable hour. Copper pots are advertised."

Paul obliged. "We've seen three letters, Alice. Maybe there are more (and likely there will be more despite my best efforts), but right now we've only got three to go on. You suggest I begin by dreaming up a hypothetical poison-pen writer, but I see the problem the other way around: there must be something we don't yet know that ties the writer's three targets together. If I can only find the link that has caused them to be confronted with a common enemy I'll have gone a long way towards identifying the letter writer."

Alice probed his theory. "And who, to your way of thinking, are the 'three targets'?"

Paul was a little disconcerted by her question. "Isn't it

obvious that it's the three men that the letters have pro-
nounced dead?"

"It isn't obvious to me. Aren't the notes also acts of
aggression against the women who received them? It can't be
pleasant receiving a message that your husband (or significant what-you-may-call-him) is dead. The first reaction may
be a terrible shock—a rush to the phone to assure yourself the
writer's wrong. And even if the recipient knows better and
avoids that moment of terror, she may toss the note out and
never mention it to anyone. In that case surely she's the only
victim. In short, Paul, whether you're hunting for malefactor
or victim, don't overlook the woman."

"I believe that's good advice."

After Alice had gone in quest of her copper pots, Paul went
through the same ritual dance he always performed before he
could bring himself to face any intellectual labors. He poured
a second cup of decaf and swept the bureau top clear to make
room for a half dozen sharp pencils, a stick of art gum (which
he preferred to erasers), a lined yellow pad, and his ubiqui-
tous spiral notebook. By the side of the notebook he placed
his Alumni Club rule book. He opened the top drawer of the
bureau and took out the football history which he'd hidden
away among his socks.

He hadn't shown the book to Alice because he hated to be
wrong. She was an unbelievably patient scholar who would
accumulate several file drawers of note cards before entrust-
ing a single word to manuscript paper. He, on the other
hand, would often proceed helter-skelter, forming and dis-
carding theories at a furious pace his researches often could
not match. Yet despite their different temperaments, Paul
assumed they must both have observed from the very outset
that there was indisputably at least one broad bond between
the author of the poison-pen notes and his three targets, and
that this bond was the Alumni Club itself. To Paul this
self-evident fact suggested a promising line of inquiry that he
had not yet been bold enough to propose to Alice. What if
the letters should not be an isolated phenomenon but only

part of a series of events that had disrupted the peace of the club?

He opened *Gridiron Glory* to the year 1916 and found a narrative of the high point of the season, the upset of heavily favored Yale. He quickly located the illustration he had expected to find. To be completely certain, he cradled the heavy volume in his arms and walked over to the picture that hung behind the bed table. Yes, it was the same, and the fuzziness of the framed print suggested it had been reproduced from the book.

Paul returned to the bureau that he had converted into his desk and read the account of the game. The key paragraph was captioned: "Benson fumble recovery leads to game-winning touchdown." It read:

> The turning point of the game against the Yale power-house led by Captain "Cupid" Black was a fumble recovery by Charlie Benson on the Yale 22-yard line with less than five minutes to go in the fourth quarter. On the very next play, reserve lineman Dick Benson caught a tackle-eligible pass and sailed unimpeded into the end zone for the winning touchdown.

Paul smiled triumphantly and consulted the club rule book. Running the membership roster under the letter "B," he stopped at the name he had checked with his pencil last evening. The man richly deserved whatever trouble he had gotten into, Paul reflected, because he was obviously a very careless reader.

Miles Corbett was dressed in his Saturday uniform, a raw-hide vest and faded blue jeans. He wore his hair (still its original comic orange) tousled and long, as if to proclaim that the "big chill" that had thinned the ranks of his sixties crowd had left him untouched. Miles's attachment to his youth was favored by nature; he was a small, sharp-featured man to whom the years had been kind. Alice had recalled this morning that Miles was the son of a president of the University. During the height of the campus antiwar protests, he had captained a sit-in at the administration building and was bodily removed from his father's office by the college police. The heroism of the moment was somewhat dimmed when his father called after him, "Don't be late for dinner, Sonny." According to the newspapers, the nickname "Sonny" had stuck to Corbett after this well-publicized incident, but you had to be a very good friend to use it to his face.

He seated Paul in a blue-painted willow easy chair and sat down opposite him on a pink-slip-covered couch strewn with large batik pillows. Paul surveyed the living room aghast. Everywhere he saw the heavy hand of an interior decorator: an antique trunk that served as a coffee table, rag rugs, plants in baskets, American primitive paintings (perhaps the work of an untalented grandchild of Grandma Moses), and a bamboo étagère housing last Christmas' art books.

After Paul and Miles had exchanged a few words, an attractive young woman walked into the room. She blended marvelously with the decor, wearing a long beige hand-woven overblouse and a pastel-striped skirt that ended in fringes at her ankles. She joined Miles on the couch.

Miles kissed her cheek, and said, "Professor Prye, let me introduce Aileen Scroop. Aileen is my interior decorator."

To leave no doubt, Aileen added, "And I like my handiwork so well, I've decided to move in with my client, as you see."

Miles turned partway to Aileen. "Professor Prye's the gentleman whom Baker's sent to us to talk about your letter."

"What do you mean, *my* letter, paleface?" Aileen replied, smiling.

"I take your point—*our* letter, I should have said."

Paul waited for the byplay to end before asking the questions he had listed in his notebook. He found they had very little to tell him that was of any value, and, to his surprise, they seemed to have very little interest in the whole matter. Neither had any theory as to who might have sent the note or why. They were inclined to think that it was just a malicious prank, but when Paul pounced on the word "malicious," neither could think of anyone connected with the club that bore them any ill will.

Paul pressed this point with Corbett. "Are there any playwrights at the club?"

"Oh yes, the University and its drama school draw the stagestruck like flies. But I've never reviewed any of their plays, if that's what you're getting at. As a matter of principle, I leave my fellow Alumni to the mercies of my junior colleagues at the *Tonsil*."

"Do you ever write articles on subjects other than drama?"

Miles nodded.

"All the time. I do feature stories on just about anything."

"Have you ever written anything about people at the Alumni Club?"

Miles inclined his head to one shoulder and clucked knowingly. "I get it, Professor Prye; in fact, I'm way ahead of you. You're looking for D'alton Mann or Edmund Yates. At last report, they were both quite dead, and I can assure you I haven't taken their place."

Paul was taken aback. He'd underestimated Corbett, who obviously had a lot more club lore at his command than he would have guessed. Colonel William D'alton Mann, the publisher of a New York scandal sheet, had been tried in 1905 for extorting "loans" from members of the Metropolitan Club under threat of exposing their disgraceful secrets in his columns. Nineteenth-century London journalist Edmund Yates had plunged the Garrick Club into turmoil by lampooning fellow member William Makepeace Thackeray.

"You seem to have an unusual mastery of club history," Paul acknowledged and hurried to change the subject.

"Are you active at the club, Mr. Corbett?"

Miles fenced with him.

"It depends what you mean. I've never held any official positions. I suppose it has been a point of honor with me since my dad, as you may know, was president of the University. I do try to help behind the scenes to keep things going smoothly. On the other hand, if your question is whether I am active socially at the club, I would have to say yes. I try to get to the major events on the club calendar when I don't run into a schedule conflict at the newspaper."

Paul decided to make one last effort to get Corbett to speculate on the "Friend"'s choice of victims.

"And you have absolutely no idea why someone would single out these three particular members as butts for what you call a 'malicious prank'?"

Corbett had nothing to add to his earlier remarks, but Aileen Scroop broke in: "Oh, but these three haven't been singled out; there have been other letters received. I can't tell you how many, but I know for sure that Melanie Ackerman got one just the other day."

"Who is Melanie Ackerman?"

Aileen responded in leisurely, pleasurable detail. Slim, long-limbed, and hennaed, Melanie Ackerman was the un-rivaled siren of the Alumni Club. Born and raised in New Orleans, she had graduated from Tulane, but taken a year's graduate study at the University in education. On the strength of that year she had become one of the first successful women applicants for membership in the Alumni Club. In the short time since she'd been admitted, clubhouse gossip had linked Melanie romantically with a remarkable number of male members, both prominent and obscure. None of her attachments seemed to last very long, and perhaps that was why they had apparently left her husband supremely unruffled.

"What's her husband like?" Paul intervened.

"Lester? He's the long-suffering husband personified. We don't see him at the club much, do we, Miles?"

Miles agreed. "That's right, and I don't know how he spends his time. There's a lot of money there, though. Before the government made us switch to registered bonds, Lester's principal occupation was probably coupon clipping. I haven't the foggiest idea what he does with himself now or where he does it."

Aileen prattled on. In her view, Melanie got on much better with men than with women, but nobody of either sex (and no matter how highly sexed) was likely to stand in her good graces consistently. Her mood swings had become legendary at the club, but fortunately she telegraphed her current emotional state. When she was feeling down, she would dress in black or dark gray, but if she appeared in any shade of red, it was best to stay out of her way; she would likely be manic, either wildly high-spirited or unbearably aggressive. In honor of the cuisine of her native Louisiana, some wag at the club had dubbed her the "black-and-red fish." Aileen commented: "Miles here blames it all on premenstrual syndrome, but of course he's so biological about everything. That's probably why I've moved in with him."

Paul gently tried to bring the conversation back to the point that interested him. "How do you know that Mrs. Ackerman received a letter from the Friend?"

"She told me so yesterday when I ran into her at the club."

"How was she dressed?" Paul asked, secretly ashamed at himself for playing Aileen's game.

"She was in dark gray, as I recall. I don't suppose these letters would put anybody in the best of spirits."

"What did the letter say?"

Aileen didn't know. "She wouldn't tell me any details, which frankly annoyed me because I had actually shown her the letter I had received."

"Do you know whether it was in the form of a condolence note?"

Aileen quickly nodded. "Yes, that much she did say, but she wouldn't even tell me which of her many men it referred to. I'm willing to bet it wasn't dear, sweet Lester."

"Do you think she'd see me?" Paul asked.

"She'd be glad to see you, I'm sure of that; she always is more than willing to see people of the male persuasion." Aileen Scroop smiled broadly without showing her teeth, like a cat with a subtle meow. "But I don't think you'll get the letter from her."

Paul involuntarily shook his head. This was going to be *some* investigation. Half of the Friend's victims probably wouldn't talk to him. The club president was on vacation. Worse than that, the letters were only part of the story and nobody (Baker included) was rushing to tell him what he didn't know. Well, he'd give it a try for a few days, and if he got nowhere he could always turn back to his history of gentlemen's clubs.

For the most part Paul's attention to Aileen's invective was simulated. According to Alice, his show of interest in conversation he found boring was less than convincing; he would tend to assume a fixed smile and gaze somewhere over the speaker's shoulder. Towards the end of Aileen's ramblings, though, she finally said something worth entering in his notebook. Occasionally interrupting her to inquire about spelling, he recorded her guesses about the identity of Melanie's Alumni Club lovers.

When he left Corbett's apartment, Paul had a hurried lunch and called Baker as arranged. Rodney had reached Vance Parry, who was now at home and willing to see Paul. Parry lived nearby in an eastside penthouse.

When Paul presented himself at Parry's door, he was greeted by one of the last of the vanishing breed of butlers and ushered into a living room with a panoramic view of the East River. The decor, in stark contrast with Aileen Scroop's creation, featured walls in gray flannel and a sectional couch in gray tweed. The room almost looked as if it had been bought from a haberdasher and needed only a striped tie to be ready for a promenade on the street below. Paul sat on a black leather Barcelona chair near a large glass table and awaited his host.

Parry soon appeared, an athletic man in his early middle years, dressed in an inevitably gray tropical suit. Paul, though, only had eyes for the woman who accompanied him, the famous Marian Morrison. Many would not have called her beautiful, but she had a strong, well-proportioned face, a forthright look, and heavy chestnut hair that fell to her shoulders in the pre-Raphaelite manner.

"I understand you want to talk to us about this stupid letter," Parry began. "I can tell you at once that it doesn't bother us at all. We've gotten used to slander, and this fellow is a piker compared to the folks that work for the major media in this town."

He looked over to Marian Morrison, who smiled her agreement. "I probably would have thrown it out," she said, "if it hadn't had this Alumni Club angle. I couldn't make sense of that at all, so I gave the letter to Vance."

"And have you figured out the club angle?" Paul asked Parry.

Parry answered with the same assurance he would have applied to the analysis of a proposed business deal.

"I don't like to downgrade the importance of what Baker's asked you to do, Mr. Prye, but I can't see a great mystery here. Do you know Baker well? If not, I should tell you he's a champion worrier, and he worries so well, you're likely to catch the habit from him if you're not careful. I think he's even given old Vic Baines the jitters; Rod tells me Vic was on your welcoming committee.

"This is the way I see it: The members who've been ridiculed in these letters are all well-known public figures. You'll forgive the immodesty in my case. Some of my publicity I could have lived without. John Richardson, of course, is the best known of the three of us, what with his Watergate fame. Sonny Corbett is still remembered from the Vietnam War protests, and I guess many people read his play reviews.

"That leaves me. I don't know whether you're interested in business news at all, Mr. Prye, but in the early days of corporate takeovers I was regarded as one of the big bad raiders. I became more respectable later, but then there was the gossip about me and Marian."

Paul wasn't sure whether Parry had finished his explanation, so he said, "That makes a lot of sense, I can see that, but why do you think the writer of these letters gave them what Ms. Morrison rightly describes as an Alumni Club angle?"

Parry was not troubled by the point. "The Alumni Club is prestigious, you know that, of course. If there's someone who doesn't like celebrities or resents the fact we've become celebrities for reasons he doesn't approve, what better place is there to embarrass us than at the club?"

Paul had to acknowledge that Parry had a point there. Why else had the Marquess of Queensberry left a note for Oscar Wilde at his club accusing him of posing as a homosexual?

"Rodney Baker makes a big deal about these letters being written by a member. That starts him worrying, as almost everything else in the world does. He's probably dead wrong, you know. It's well known that Richardson, Corbett, and I are members of the Alumni Club. We've been pictured in the press at club functions on many occasions. So just about anyone in New York who reads knows we won't be delighted to receive unpleasant letters on Alumni Club stationery.

"Marian and I aren't sure that the writer is a member of the club at all. The stationery is available at desks all over the club premises, and anyone could walk off the street and take a supply with no trouble. But I shouldn't speak for Marian, Mr. Prye. You may not know this, but Marian's a University graduate. She joined the Alumni Club early this year."

Marian smiled at Paul and looked directly into his eyes as she spoke. "I agree with Vance completely. Rodney's making far too much out of a minor nuisance."

Paul pretended to make a dutiful entry in his notebook and turned back to Vance Parry. "I think I forgot to ask whether you've ever been an officer of the club."

Parry answered quickly, treading on Paul's last words. "Oh, no, that's not my style at all. I don't see myself heading up the Games Committee. I do try to help out when I can, but without fanfare."

Helps out without fanfare, Paul wrote. What had Corbett said? "Behind the scenes."

"Of course," Parry continued, "with our financial head-ache at the Company, I haven't had much time for club problems lately."

Paul was much too polite to be cut out for private investigation; he had sat here all this time waiting for Parry to mention the bankruptcy.

"You don't suppose, do you," he ventured, "that it's your business problem that's behind Ms. Morrison's letter?"

Parry remained silent, but Marian Morrison answered without any apparent constraint:

"It'd never have occurred to us, frankly. What do you have in mind?"

"Well," Paul paused. "I was wondering whether any of your major creditors or shareholders are members of the Alumni Club."

Marian maintained her intense eye contact. "I can't think of any creditors; at least there's nobody at the club from the creditors' committee. The way those characters are giving us orders these days, I'd have to guess they all went to West Point. Shareholders are another story, there must be many among our club members. Parry Enterprises shares are widely held, as you must know. But in any event, our shareholders have been very supportive." As an afterthought she added lightly, "At least judging from letters the Com-pany gets from shareholders, all of whom, by the way, sign their names."

If Marian Morrison is right in believing the bankruptcy's not the reason for their letter and if Parry's theory is sound, Paul thought, there must be a "celebrity" involved somehow with Melanie Ackerman. Without revealing the ground of his curiosity, he asked his hosts what they knew of her. Parry didn't display the slightest interest, but perhaps it was once again that Marian Morrison was answering for both of them:

"Melanie can be a pain, that's what Vance's silence is telling you politely. Still, she's nobody's fool, you'd see that in a few minutes' conversation. The problem is she's never found her subject, whether it's work, community activity, children, whatever. So she falls back on the old ways of getting ahead."

"And what's that?"

"In a word, pleasing. She's a compulsive flirt, many say it's something more than that, she's got a bad reputation at the club. But I'm not sure it's deserved. I've suffered myself from loose tongues, so I'm slow to judge."

Slow as she might be, she did not hesitate for a moment when Paul asked if she would write a list of Melanie's rumored conquests at the club. She wrote diligently while Parry filled the time with courteous small talk about the weather and George Steinbrenner's most recent quarrels with his Yankees. When Marian handed Paul her compilation at last, Paul gave it a quick glance that assured him she had not erred on the side of omission. There were two details that immediately caught his eye. Either Marian had given the subject a great deal of thought in the past or she had a extraordinarily orderly memory, for she had without hesitation written the names in perfect alphabetical order. The second point was even stranger: not a single name on her list overlapped with the roster he had been given with supreme confidence by Aileen Scroop.

When Paul found that Alice had returned to their room ahead of him, he observed with relief that there were no copper pots in evidence. "The flea market was terrible," Alice said gloomily, "except that on the way out I found an irresistible art-nouveau buckle. I think it's a butterfly, or perhaps a pretentious moth. How do you vote?" She freed the insect from its tissue paper and awaited his judgment.

"If it cost you a penny more than five dollars, it must be a butterfly."

As she dressed, Paul told her about the day's interviews. She was unimpressed by what he had learned.

"Are you beginning to get the feeling that the Alumni are pulling your leg?"

Paul looked up from the club rule book which he was casually scanning. "Why do you say that?"

Continuing to concentrate her full critical faculties on the progress of her cosmetics, Alice answered,

"Is it credible to you that all these people—Rod Baker and Vic Baines included—simply have no notion at all who the Friend is or what he's up to? Not even to the point of training the beady eyes of Gridlock Holmes in a promising direction?"

Only recently had Alice bestowed on Paul the nickname "Gridlock Holmes." It was in mild protest against his habit of expounding his solutions of baffling nineteenth-century crimes while their car was hopelessly caught in the summer's horrendous weekend traffic.

"Why wouldn't they want to help me?" Paul asked.

She was unmoved by the question. "That's for you to find out. You're the investigator, I'm just a consulting genius."

"But why would Baker have invited us here and why would Corbett and Parry see me if they didn't want me to succeed?"

Alice was ready to dismiss the subject. "Maybe somebody told them to."

About a half hour later the Pryes emerged from the elevator and picked their way past the grillroom tables towards the Great Hall. Alice was dressed in an antique thirties chiffon with floating godets that worried Paul. He followed at a respectful distance; one evening when they were rushing to leave home, he had stepped on her hem, converting her on the spot into a semi-nude descending a staircase. He had never heard the end of it; and, worse than that, they'd been late for the opera. She waited for him to catch up with her under the Hall's wide archway and whispered, "Remember, Paul, you're here to do some sleuthing. Don't just hover over the bowl of cashews."

He nodded inattentively, because his eye had been caught by a wall plaque to the right of the archway:

BAINESGATE
This enlarged archway is named in honor of the tenth
anniversary of Victor Baines' dedicated service as Chairman of the House Committee.
August 1, 1985.

The Great Hall was only sparsely filled. There apparently
wasn't going to be much of a crowd turning out to shake the
hands of the new members on this uncomfortably muggy
night. Rodney Baker spotted the Pryes after a few moments
and made a round of listless introductions. Most of the
people they met were new members or club functionaries; it
seemed to Paul that their spouses had generally declined to
come (or perhaps had not been invited). Baker brought the
Pryes at last to meet Ralph Murray, chairman of the Admissions Committee, which was hosting the affair, and a long-
jawed man with a self-mocking smile who stood at his side.
"And this is Brian Kennedy," Baker said as he retreated. "I'm
sure you'll enjoy each other."

Brian indicated pretty early that he would enjoy Alice a lot
more than Paul and guided her towards the hors d'oeuvres.
Paul, left alone with Murray, groped for an ice breaker. "I
have a friend who's applied to the Alumni Club. I wonder
whether he's among the new members."

"What's his name?" Murray did not seem much more
comfortable than Paul with cocktail conversation.

"Professor Ben Tolliver."

Murray stiffened and did not answer at once. He then
gathered his forces and said, "The name did not come before
us. Perhaps Professor Tolliver changed his mind and withdrew his application."

Another faux pas to add to the list for which Paul Prye was
famous. Thank God Alice wasn't there to witness his embarrassment. Ben Tolliver would never have withdrawn his
name, Paul was certain of that. The Alumni Club had not
forgotten that ridiculous student harassment case.

From this unpromising beginning Paul turned the conversation to the Friend's letters. Murray was aware that a few members had received them, but he seemed very indifferent to what he plainly regarded as a minor disturbance of club decorum. He would be glad to talk to Paul, though; Baker had mentioned that he'd requested Paul to make discreet inquiries and had asked the committees to cooperate with him. Murray invited Paul to meet him for lunch on Monday at his Wall Street firm's executive dining room. They usually had a first-rate red snapper on Monday, with a sauce that he was glad to say was not *nouvelle cuisine*.

"Thanks a lot. May I ask you a couple of questions before I leave you to your guests?"

"Of course."

"Who handles 'elimination' of club members?"

Murray looked suspicious. "You mean for nonpayment of dues?"

"Or other matters," Paul said noncommittally.

"Generally it's our committee that's responsible for recommending expulsions—or, as you put it, 'eliminations,' but I'm afraid that word sounds more like the Hell's Angels than the Alumni Club. The president and trustees make all final decisions."

When Murray walked off, Paul entered his Monday lunch date in his notebook. He then went off in search of Alice and found her talking with Brian Kennedy at the hors d'oeuvres table and in fact standing not very far away from the cashew bowl she had instructed him to avoid.

Alice and Brian were happily engaged in repartee, so Paul decided to comfort himself with overeating. As he began to pile his plate with shrimps and oysters, he heard a great commotion coming from the entrance to the Great Hall. His first impression that the women had stayed home was no longer correct if it had ever been, for high-pitched voices dominated the tumult at the archway. A large group had gathered there to greet a new arrival with a collective fervor usually reserved for royalty and rock superstars.

Before the Pryes could ask, Rodney Baker arrived with the explanation: "Paul and Alice, come meet our newest member, Thomas Simmons." He led them through the crush at the entrance.

Paul blinked self-consciously, afraid that he had been about to stare. It was (strange to say, considering his preoccupation with violent crime), the first time Paul had ever been brought face to face with a convicted killer. Simmons was not quite so tall as he had appeared on television, when testifying with great fluency or joking easily with reporters during the recesses. But the deep suntan was the same (even more impressive than on their RCA), as were the trim outdoorsman's build, the deep charismatic blue eyes, and the elegant high forehead. A henna-haired young woman, smiling with an abundance of gum, hung on his arm. She was dressed in a bright-red knit that clashed with her hair; a black patent leather "feed bag" was slung over her shoulder. Paul involuntarily summoned up an incongruous image from his crime scrapbooks: John Dillinger and the mysterious "woman in red" who betrayed him to the FBI.

Baker made the introductions. "Tom, I'd like you to meet my guests at the club, Paul and Alice Prye. Paul and Alice, Tom Simmons."

Simmons' companion protested. "Rodney, what bad manners you have. Aren't you going to introduce me?" Perhaps "companion" was the wrong word. It wasn't apparent whether she had come in with Simmons or had merely been the first of his female admirers to claim him on arrival.

"Sorry about that," Rodney said. "Paul and Alice, this is Melanie Ackerman."

The Pryes were muttering their hellos when they heard Brian Kennedy's jeering voice close by. "Melanie, long time no see. How's Lester?"

"Oh, he's off again on one of his foolish camping weekends." She detached herself from Simmons and treated Kennedy to a swooping embrace.

Despite what he'd heard of Melanie from Aileen Scroop and Marian Morrison, Paul thought that anyone who didn't like camping couldn't be all bad. He'd never understood his adventurous friends who only went on tours where there were no roads and they could be knee-deep in something or other. Alice had dubbed these excursions "Club Mud."

Simmons' welcoming crowd had fallen back a little but not to disperse. Instead they ringed an area near the Hall entrance where the Pryes and Rodney Baker stood near the celebrity member.

"I'm pleased to meet you, Professor Prye," Simmons said, "in fact, I couldn't be more delighted. I found your commentary in the *Times* about my trial most interesting and in many ways very acute. I suspect, though, if I may say it without giving offense, that you probably don't know much about the loading of pistols."

"You are quite right about that, Mr. Simmons. You have me at a disadvantage there. I've never fired a handgun."

The blow did not land, or at least it did not register. Simmons went on: "I found your remarks on my prison book especially perceptive, though I did regret your suggestion that the publishing profits should have passed to my wife's estate under the Son of Sam law. I had hoped at least to make it clear that my main purpose in writing the book was to comment on prison conditions and not to capitalize on the public interest in my trial for the shooting accident."

Alice was enjoying the battle and decided to make it a tag-team match. "I thought, Mr. Simmons, that Paul's comments on the book were largely favorable. I seem to recall his saying that your prison letters showed a fine epistolary style."

Paul gave Alice a pained look. Perhaps he was doing her an injustice but he wondered whether she was trying to join him in playing detective. In any event, Simmons didn't react to her words, and perhaps he was not yet aware of the anonymous letters. He did, however, address his next words to her: "What is your work, Mrs. Prye? There was some reference in your husband's bio at the end of the article, but it's slipped my mind."

"I am an art historian."

"Oh yes, I remember that now." He gave her an appraising

look that implied expertise. "Do you know what the amo-
rous female art lecturer says in the dark?"

"I've no idea," said Alice unobligingly.

"Next slide, please."

Alice didn't flinch. "That's a Woody Allen variant." She
was always quick to supply a footnote.

"An improvement surely," Simmons replied.

Is this the famous "charm" of which we've heard so much?
Alice wondered with disgust. If so, it was not compounded
of wit or grace but of a studied insouciance and an indifference to social convention.

Melanie Ackerman, having finished her conversation with
Kennedy, came back to claim Simmons. She took his hand
and swung it gaily, beaming into his face. *"Thomas,"* she
said, lingering over the first syllable as if teaching him his
own name, "what a sweaty palm you have, just like a
nervous schoolboy. Are you quite overcome by the honor
the Alumni Club has bestowed on you?" Her smile stayed.

"No, it is by the honor of your company," Simmons said,
correctly reading her thought.

Without releasing his hand, Melanie took the role of a
stand-up talk-show hostess and began to barrage him with
questions. Did he think he'd come to the club much? Or was
his membership merely the final seal of approval on his
return to society? Didn't he agree with her that the Admissions Committee had acted in a truly *professional* manner,
putting aside all extraneous considerations? It was plain to
Alice that Melanie was not the slightest bit interested in his
answers, perhaps not even expecting any. She was putting on
a performance for the Pryes and for the many members who
still clustered around Simmons, and was bent on demonstrat-
ing her social ease with the club's new lion.

Before Melanie could complete her inquisition, the lights
suddenly failed, pitching the Hall into total darkness.

"It's that damn air-conditioning again," Paul whispered to
Alice. "What do you say we sneak back to the International?"

"Or better still, go home and help the painters," Alice
suggested.

Near the doorway an invisible comedian shouted, "Here's hoping Tom Simmons isn't toting his forty-four tonight." Paul thought he recognized Brian Kennedy's voice.

The lights were soon restored. After arranging meetings with Victor Baines (whose suit was the same wilting navy) and Brian Kennedy (who, he had learned from the rule book, was chairman of the Athletics and Games Committee), Paul guided Alice back to the open bar for a last drink. The party was breaking up, and a parade of mixed couples was beginning to pass through the archway into the main dining room where a refectory table had been set for club dignitaries and their spouses to entertain a select company of the new members. The Pryes stood aside to allow the procession to go by, Rodney Baker at its head. Paul saw Miles Corbett escorting Aileen Scroop, Vance Parry chatting with Marian Morrison, and Melanie Ackerman with her arm possessively encircling Tom Simmons' waist. The strikingly handsome Ralph Murray stood at the foot of the long table beckoning his guests to find their places and missing no opportunity to show off his profile.

Losing interest in the dinner party, Paul asked Alice what she thought of the notorious Tom Simmons.

"A boor, don't you think? He seems perfectly suited, though, to Melanie Ackerman. What do you call a female boor?"

Paul had never considered the question, so Alice continued, "Simmons is probably about what we could have expected, but the fawning Alumni really get to me. They're the kind that must think every middle-class murderer is entitled to one freebie."

They drifted to other subjects and were about to settle the serious business of their evening plans. Paul earnestly advocated the off-Broadway revival of *The Mystery of Edwin Drood*.

His back was to the dining room but Alice was looking past him towards the table of honor. She stopped Paul in mid-sentence: "Look, Paul. Something's going on."

Many of the Admissions Committee's guests had risen

abruptly from the table, scraping their chairs on the dark oak floor. They fell apart into a number of contending groups, faces contorted with rage, fists clenched or fingers pointing, shouting accusations at each other in total disregard of the startled looks of the other diners in the well-filled room. Alice saw Ralph Murray standing in the midst of the combatants, arms outstretched to calm their fury. In secret amusement she saw him as a modern male reincarnation of Hersilia attempting to pacify the warriors in David's *Sabine Women*. Perhaps it was his classical face.

Murray's peacemaking, unlike Hersilia's, was a failure. Several couples strode angrily from the dining room, leaving only a sparse remnant at the refectory table. The Pryes lingered in the Great Hall until the commotion had died down, and then slipped unobtrusively into the front lobby. There they found Rodney Baker in earnest conversation with Victor Baines.

"What in the world's going on back there?" Paul asked.

"Something very odd," Rodney said. "It was the place cards. A number of the guests were unhappy with the seating."

"And why were they unhappy?" Paul felt that he was pulling teeth.

"Well, you see, many of them found themselves sitting next to a former"—he groped for a word even trustees could use—"love interest."

"How very romantic," Alice intervened. "Your Mr. Murray must be quite a joker."

Rodney shook his head. "No, that's just the thing that has us all so puzzled. Someone must have switched the place cards."

CHAPTER 4

Paul didn't sleep well Saturday night. He'd voted for the wrong villain in *The Mystery of Edwin Drood* and Alice had been triumphantly right. Then the zakuski and borscht at the Russian Tea Room had been more than a match for his digestion.

At 6:30 A.M. he quietly got out of his bed and mixed an overdose of decaf, hoping the 3 percent caffeine or whatever it was would multiply to a strength sufficient to open his eyes. After he felt semiconscious, he stumbled across the room to find the briefcase that contained the notes on his book. He then pulled the chair to the window so that he could read by the morning light without disturbing Alice.

The subfile he had before him was labeled "Club Hostilities." Turning the pages of his summary, he read:

> Roland Burnham Molineux. Molineux was the central figure in what remains New York clubland's most sensational crime. In 1898 he murdered a member of the Knickerbocker Athletic Club and attempted to kill a club employee (dispatching an elderly relative instead) by anonymous mailings of patent medicines laced with cyanide. The lethal packages were mailed to the in-

tended victims at the club, of which Molineux had been a member until he resigned a year before.

Molineux's grievances against the two men were apparently unrelated. His first victim, H. C. Barnet, had been his rival for the hand of Blanche Chesebrough, whom Molineux married shortly after Barnet's death. Harry Cornish, to whom he mailed the second package of poison, was the athletic director of the club, whom Molineux had unsuccessfully sought to have ousted from his post. Cornish had offended Molineux, the club's champion gymnast, by refusing to order his favored brand of horizontal bars and by permitting guests to use improper language at the swimming pool. When the club's board rejected his complaints, he resigned in protest (or defeat).

A curious feature of the case is that before the poisonings Molineux established fictitious letter-box accounts in the names of his future victims through which he conducted correspondence with drug firms advertising cures for impotency. It is significant that in so doing he had appropriated his enemies' personalities before he made an attack on their lives. He treated them, in short, as if they were already dead.

Paul had no quarrel with what he had written, but as he lay half-awake last night, he had had some further thoughts. In the margin of the page he had been reading he made these supplementary comments:

> There's a tantalizing riddle here about motivation. Molineux's grudge against Barnet couldn't have been more personal. But would he have killed him if his brain had not first been overheated with club vendettas? Why else would he have devised a plan to murder Barnet *at the club?* And why would he invent a common scheme to eliminate a rival wooer and the athletic director? Is not the answer possibly this—that his true victim in both cases was the Knickerbocker Club, which would be identified forever with these twin tragedies?

Paul was not confident that he'd unmask the Friend from the Alumni Club, but perhaps this comfortably minor mystery had given him new insight into the Molineux puzzle. At least so it had seemed to him early in the morning, before he had exposed his theory to Alice's shrewd objections or, still worse, to the withering examination of Detective Lieutenant Dave Emmerich, whom they had invited for Sunday brunch at a café in SoHo. It was nothing but habit that brought the Pryes back to this popular Sunday haunt, where New Yorkers docilely tried to digest thickly sliced French toast and downed G-rated Bloody Marys.

The Pryes met Emmerich at ten o'clock. Paul had been fortified by the French toast, and generous servings of butter and syrups, before he broached his new thoughts on the Molineux case.

Dave grunted politely but brought the conversation back to the twentieth century. "I'm a tough guy during the week but never on Sundays, particularly with friends who are picking up the tab. I don't agree with you, but let's forget Molineux and the Knickerbocker. It closed long ago, anyway. Tell me more about what's going on at the Alumni Club."

Paul had given him a brief rundown on the phone this morning, but now he and Alice filled in the details, beginning with Rodney Baker's surprising commission and ending with the fracas at the refectory table.

"Let's take a look at those letters," Dave requested.

Paul handed him additional Xerox copies he'd had made. He also gave him the brown envelope containing the originals Baker had delivered that morning, and the three pens he had removed from the writing desks.

Dave was unimpressed by the letters. "Nonsense, if you ask me. It's no wonder the club hasn't called the police, but what I'm surprised at is that they'd bother you."

"Well, you know us academics." Paul caught the unconscious note of professional superiority. "We have nothing in particular to do with our summers."

Dave overlooked the jab. "I'll have the pens and ink tested

against the letters, as you've asked. But I'm not sure I see
what we'll prove if they match up."

"Probably not an awful lot. But, Dave, according to the
rule book, there are about thirty-two hundred current members. Anything that can help us cut down the universe in
which we can locate the Friend is a step forward. So my
thought was this: Suppose we can show that these letters, or
some of them, were or could have been written at a writing
desk on the main floor or the gallery of the club. I'd wonder
whether the Friend is not then likely to be someone who'd
feel at ease writing—or, more to the point, being seen
writing—in a public area of the club. Someone who's there a
good deal of the time."

"Why couldn't the Friend have written the letters in one of
the guest rooms?"

"It seems doubtful that a nonresident member would
know so much about the New Yorkers mentioned in the
letters or would have had an opportunity to collect the
grievances that are behind this correspondence. Then we also
have the evidence of the Scroop and Morrison lists."

Paul offered Emmerich copies of Marian's alphabetical
roster of Melanie Ackerman's reported lovers and of his
transcription of Aileen Scroop's alternative speculation, but
Dave turned them down. "I don't mind the lab tests, but I
really can't get into any personalities unless we're called in.
Parlor games are not our line."

Paul looked disappointed, but Alice didn't want the conversation cut short just when it finally showed promise of
turning scandalous.

"What do the lists tell us? I recognize some of the names,
of course."

Paul scored a little victory; it was one of the discoveries
he'd held back. "Almost everyone on both lists is a club
official."

"So what?" Alice felt cheated. "How do we know that the
club rumors are true, or that these women aren't settling old
scores of their own? Remember what you told me about
Aileen's smile? Also, Paul, wasn't it Aileen's guess that one of

Melanie's lovers was the man attacked in her letter, not the sender?"

"Maybe she was wrong."

Alice persisted. "Besides, we don't even know it to be a fact that Melanie actually received a letter from the Friend."

"You're right there," Paul conceded. "I'll ask her."

Alice responded quickly. "If you do, Gridlock, you're taking me along."

On Monday morning Paul started his round of committee interviews with a seven-thirty call to his friend, Harry Fowler, a member of the Wine and Food Committee. The early hour was not a matter of diligence; Paul had no choice. Harry was a psychoanalyst with a routine that in his own case he called "fixed" but in his patients would have found "compulsive." He set his first appointment at eight-thirty in the morning and ended his labors eleven hours and fifty minutes later.

Paul told Harry of Alice's MSG attack and mentioned his theory that one of the special house wines had done the trick. There was a moment of silence as Harry struggled with his shock; he was a chevalier in an international order of wine connoisseurs. "Do you remember what the wine was?"

"I'm not sure we were ever told the name. It was an Italian regional of some kind; the steward described it as a kissing cousin to Barolo. Have you been serving it long?"

"No, as a matter of fact, the whole notion of serving house wines by the glass is a recent innovation; it was a recommendation of our new food-service manager. But I'm finding it hard to accept your explanation of Alice's allergic reaction. It's very unusual to find MSG in wine. I remember several years ago having some complaints along that line concerning our Spanish wines, where we suspected the exporter of trying to mask some mislabeled Algerian. I hope our Italian suppliers aren't playing the same games. We'll certainly look into it at once."

The chairman of the Wine and Food Committee was a

chemist for a preserved-foods trade association, Harry explained; he had his own home equipment for measuring alcohol and sugar content of the club's wines and for detecting the admixture of flavor boosters. The New York City importers had called on him as a consultant in the crisis that arose a few years ago over contaminants in Austrian and Italian wines.

"I'll be interested in your chairman's findings," Paul said, "and if he discovers a high MSG level, I'd like to hear his views on how the adulteration could have occurred."

Harry was alarmed. "I trust you're not suggesting we tamper with our wines at the club."

"I make no suggestion at all, Harry, but strange things are going on at the club these days. Tell me, though, how are the house wines bottled?"

"Sometimes in gallon bottles, more often in half-gallons."

"And what kind of seals do the bottles have?"

"I believe they would have screw-on caps. You don't usually find corks in these bulk wine bottles. The wines are not high quality, you understand, and in any case they probably contain some preservatives."

Paul referred to his notebook. "Harry, I don't remember whether I asked you where the Italian regionals are stored."

"They're kept in the wine cellar, except for a few bottles that are in current use. Those would be kept behind the bar."

"Where are the keys to the wine cellar kept?"

"I haven't any idea. You know our committee doesn't serve the wine, we just consult about its selection."

Paul was tempted to give his opinion about how well the committee was discharging this function, but he restrained himself. Instead, Paul chatted a bit about the Alumni's taste in wine and then introduced a new subject. "What can you tell me about Rodney Baker's activity at the club?"

"Rodney, oh, he's a big wheel there, as I suppose he is at every organization he's interested in. Why do you ask?"

"Rodney's asked me to do something for the club, it's a matter of a confidential nature. What I want to be clear on is whether he would be authorized to speak for the club."

"If that's your worry, Paul, set your mind at rest. Rod Baker *is* the Alumni Club."

"What about Victor Baines?"

"He's a fixture on the House Committee, but he doesn't have Baker's influence."

Paul frowned. "It's strange, though, that the club book doesn't show Baker's name in any official capacity."

"That's not the way Rod works and, I might add, that's not the way the club works either. I'd bet a pile that Rod's on the Oversight Committee."

"What's the Oversight Committee? I didn't see it mentioned among the committee listings."

"That must be an oversight," Harry joked feebly, "maybe that's how the committee got its name. But official titles have nothing to do with how power is exercised at the Alumni Club. In fact, our current president's year is equally divided into two parts, a summer vacation followed almost immediately by a winter vacation. It's the Oversight Committee that runs the show. Nobody elects them, nobody fires them, and, in fact, not very many people even know who they are. But I'm pretty sure Rodney Baker is one of them, and if there is a little supercabinet that oversees the Oversight Committee, you can rest assured that Rodney Baker's on that as well.

"In short, Paul, don't lose any sleep about Rodney Baker lacking clout at the club. But now, if you'll excuse me, our fifty minutes are up."

Paul didn't know whether it was another attempt at humor or the words had just slipped out.

An incurably early man, Paul Prye arrived at the Wall Street offices of Carter & Sons almost twenty minutes early for his appointment with Ralph Murray. He seated himself opposite the reception desk in a low soft leather armchair from which he expected to have trouble rising. On the wall behind the receptionist was a turn-of-the-century portrait of a man in a frock coat looking benevolently down at a world globe. It was the founder, he presumed, Mr. Carter, contemplating the international securities market.

As he waited, Paul reflected that Ralph Murray was going to be a tough nut to crack. He'd been polite enough in agreeing to the interview, but Paul had sensed a strong reserve when he touched on the subject of expulsion of members. Yet it was an inevitable question if he was to make any headway.

History had shown that group rejection could cause more dire consequences than facetious condolences. There was the celebrated example of the crimes committed by the Austrian lieutenant Hofrichter after he was denied admission to the military elite. Shortly before Christmas of 1909, the lieutenant attempted to poison a number of officers recently admitted to the General Staff by mailing them "nerve-strengthening" pills containing cyanide; one of his victims died. At first Vienna was shocked by the apparently purposeless crime, but it was eventually brought home to Hofrichter, whose own candidacy for the General Staff had been unsuccessful.

Then, too, there was the case of Fighting Fitzgerald . . .

Paul's thoughts were interrupted at this point by the appearance of Ralph Murray's secretary, who ushered him directly into the firm's executive dining suite. She seated him at a small table in one of the many alcoves off the main room that were obviously intended for confidential conversations. Paul thought uncharitably that these private nooks were just the place for discreet exchanges of "inside information." In a few minutes Ralph Murray joined him, resplendent in a green tie patterned with the firm's logo and a matching handkerchief professionally folded in his breast pocket. The green had not faded despite Black Monday. After a prelude of small talk, Murray strongly renewed his recommendation of the red snapper, to which Paul acceded.

Paul found that the fish was justly praised and between forkfuls pursued his inquiry:

"Mr. Murray, I've read the club rules on admissions and find them a bit puzzling."

"And why is that?"

Paul opened his already dog-eared rule book for reference. "Well, on the face of things, it looks like anyone who's graduated from the University or attended postgraduate courses is qualified for membership."

"That is correct."

Paul continued. "And yet before the application can be approved, the candidate must be interviewed by two members of your committee and notice of his candidacy must also be posted on the club bulletin board. What's the point of all these procedures if ultimately the only issue is whether the applicant studied at the University?"

Murray paused for a moment to take a drink of iced tea. "I think it would be an overstatement to say that the University connection is the only issue, Professor Prye. We are, after all, a club, and we want to satisfy ourselves that the man would get along, that he would be—"

Paul helped him. "I think the word used to be 'clubbable.' But how important is it for a man to be clubbable at an urban alumni club with over three thousand members?"

"I don't think that's a completely fair question. You know, we don't usually meet en masse. We often see each other in small social settings, across a card table, for example, or on the squash courts. We think that we're justified therefore in wanting to form some impression of the applicant's personality and his reputation. Also, although I don't think anyone would call us intolerant of different life-styles, we are old-fashioned—I'm not ashamed to say it—and we do look for new members who will be comfortable with the club rules."

Paul readily agreed. "I know what you mean; I'm afraid I've violated several of those rules already and we've only been there a few days. But these personal factors you mentioned; how often do they lead you to reject an application?"

Murray looked a little offended. "Oh, we never reject an application."

"I'm afraid you've lost me there," Paul said, wondering whether he'd been having difficulty following Murray's explanation.

"Well, you see, Professor Prye, if the committee begins to have the feeling that a candidate is running into trouble, we call the principal sponsor and suggest that the application be withdrawn."

Paul thought this a minor procedural quibble at best but pretended to be impressed by the distinction. "Well, how many applications would you guess have run into trouble within the past year?"

Murray squirmed in his chair, as if he were suffering from an insect bite. At length he said, "Oh, I would say no more than a few."

"And would you be willing to give me the names of the candidates?"

Murray declined emphatically. "That would be inappropriate, Professor Prye. Our committee proceedings must be completely confidential, as I am sure you will understand."

"Well, would I be guessing correctly that my friend Ben Tolliver is one of the unsuccessful applicants?"

Murray met his gaze squarely. "I will have to let my last answer stand."

"What if I were to renew this inquiry through Rodney Baker?"

Paul had finished the succulent red snapper and had only a bit of coffee left, so he was perhaps more willing to risk a sudden termination of the interview.

"I'll face the issue with Mr. Baker if and when it ever arises." Ralph Murray would not be much of a chairman if he had not learned how to put off the evil day, so Paul abruptly changed course:

"Well, what can you tell me about the expulsion of Charles Benson the Fourth?"

Taken by surprise, Murray blurted out: "How in the world did you learn about that?"

Without giving his host a chance to recover his composure, Paul rushed forward with his explanation: "I'm not Sherlock Holmes but I'm not a complete incompetent either. On our arrival at the club we were assigned to room 759. It is a newly refurbished room and I determined from last year's annual report that the room decorations were the gift of a new member, Charles Benson IV. You may wonder why I troubled to look into that fact. Well, it was obvious to me that the club had found something fishy about Mr. Benson's gift. Some of the photographs—probably of the exploits of predecessor Bensons—had been removed from the wall and a door plaque that undoubtedly had memorialized Charles Benson's generosity had been taken off the front door; the imprint of the door plate can still be felt under the heavy varnish.

"Now the people who wanted to erase all signs of Mr. Benson's endowment of our room made a mistake, at least I think they did. You see, there's a little football photograph still on the wall. It isn't very conspicuous because it's partly hidden by our night-table lamp. Maybe it was left hanging because it escaped attention. But then again, perhaps not. It is a genuine picture of a key play in the 1916 football team's victory over Yale. In fact, the only thing wrong with it is a slight error in the caption due to Charlie the Fourth's hasty reading of the University's football history. He said the photo showed Charlie Benson running for a touchdown against Yale. In fact, as I found from consulting the University's football chronicles, Charlie Benson did play a crucial role by recovering a Yale fumble, but it was another Benson—a reserve player—who later carried the ball in for a touchdown. Funny how the same family names keep cropping up on the sports rosters of the early Eastern teams. It's like reading Chinese history."

Murray remained silent, so Paul proceeded to finish his explanation: "The fact is that there is a graduate of the University named Charles Benson the Fourth. So I was told when I called the Alumni office this morning, but the real Benson is alive and well and living in Seattle. He seemed quite a pleasant fellow and didn't mind when I roused him from bed at 7 A.M., having completely forgotten the three-hour time difference, as I tend to do. He rarely comes to New York, he tells me, and has never visited the Alumni Club.

"So it's my conclusion, Mr. Murray, that the club member who decorated our room for the class of 1916 was an impostor; that he filled the walls with instant ancestors or the like; that someone found him out; that his fake memorabilia were removed from the room; and that your committee probably ejected him from the club. Am I right so far?"

Murray looked at his watch as if hoping to rescue himself with the excuse of another appointment. If this was his idea, he thought better of it. "It has been an embarrassment we have had trouble keeping under wraps, so I can say you are essentially correct."

"How did the matter come to light?"

Murray shrugged. "I'm a little vague about that now. It all goes back a few months. I seem to recall someone on the House Committee telling us that some of the pictures weren't right and that we should look into the matter."

"Were you informed by the chairman?"

"Vic Baines? It could have been him, that certainly would have been the right channel. But I simply can't recall."

"Who was it that advised Benson of his expulsion?"

"It was I," Murray answered quickly, "that was my unpleasant responsibility."

Although he realized that he was probing a sore point, Paul went further: "How did you break it to him, and what was his reaction?"

It was apparent that Murray didn't want to say much more. "To your second question I must say I have no idea. I wrote him a letter in behalf of my committee and the club president stating merely that a review of his credentials indicated he was not qualified for continued membership. I enclosed a pro-rata refund of his current dues. And now, Professor Prye, I must ask you to excuse me."

Belatedly Murray referred to the pressure of another engagement.

The cocktail hour with Victor Baines was a letdown after the red snapper served up by Carter & Sons. Paul found Baines waiting for him at the designated restaurant bar, over which hung a spacious blond nude of the genus Helga. Sucking at his meerschaum, Baines had already downed half a glass of some kind of whiskey he was drinking on the rocks. Near his glass was an untouched plate of dreary canapés he had ordered in anticipation of Paul's arrival. Paul shook hands and slid onto the corner stool at Baines' right. They were alone at the bar except for a young woman in a dark suit and a blouse with the obligatory yuppie bow; sitting a few places away, she eyed them with interest and apparently threatened to hang on every word.

"What'll it be, Professor Prye?" Baines inquired.

"Scotch on the rocks."

"Any brand in particular?"

His mind on the coming interview, Paul shook his head. "No, anything they have will do." Baines ordered him a Glenfiddich, his own favorite, and when the bartender returned with the drink, he nudged the plate of appetizers in Paul's direction. "Sorry about this wretched fare, but it's the best a poor widower can offer." He then put his pipe aside and asked,

"What's new since Saturday, Professor Prye? Have you made any progress on our club's little mystery?"

"You mean the anonymous letters? No, I can't claim much success on that front so far, but the fact is I've become even more interested in quite a different mystery, Mr. Baines."

"Shall we do Vic and Paul?"

"Of course."

"Well then, Paul, what's your favorite mystery now?"

"The mystery of Room 759." He was embarrassed as the phrase came out; it sounded like the title of an old French thriller. "You see, that's the room we've been given, and I—"

Vic Baines interrupted him. "And being a clever man, you've somehow—and with incredible speed, it seems to me—uncovered the Charlie Benson affair."

Paul told him what he had learned.

"Careless of us to leave the football photo," Baines said, signaling the bartender for a refill. "But no harm done. We haven't gone out of our way to publicize the matter, but it's not a state secret either. I sometimes wish our committee members were a bit more discreet."

"How did you first learn your Benson was an impostor?"

"Well, I suppose it had to come out sometime. The fellow just couldn't leave well enough alone. He wasn't satisfied with slipping a falsified application past the Admissions Committee. No sooner was he admitted than he volunteered to help furnish your room in behalf of the class of 1916, whose sports superstar had been Charlie Benson the Second. And he really did a great job. Somehow he was able to come up with reproductions of genuine Benson family photos. But apparently he's a man who always has to gild the lily, so he also contributed a framed letter of gratitude from Mayor LaGuardia to Charlie the Second.

"After the renovations on the seventh floor were finished, we had an open house one Sunday to show off the new rooms. This turned out to be our fraudulent Benson's undoing. Among the visitors to Room 759 was an elderly member who'd known the Benson family quite well. He immediately spotted the LaGuardia letter as a fake; it seems that the mayor and Charlie the Second had been mortal enemies. From that point on the whole house of cards collapsed. We had the Admissions Committee look more thoroughly into the background of the man who called himself Charlie Benson the Fourth. As you've learned yourself, there is in fact an alum by that name, but he was unfortunately not our member."

"And when was Charlie the pretender ejected from the club?"

Vic Baines replied without pausing for recollection. "It was posted on April first of this year. I remember a lot of silly April Fool jokes that ran around the club—at the expense of both our committees."

Paul declined Vic's offer of a second drink. "What sort of man was Charlie?"

"I met him a few times, but couldn't form much of an impression. I didn't get into the nitty-gritty of the room renovations. We left that to the club staff."

"Do you know where he is now?"

"I haven't the vaguest idea. He was a resident member, and

you could get his mailing address from the accounting office. Of course, it's possible he's moved away since we expelled him. It must have been very embarrassing for him; it certainly was for us. I do know, though, that he still shows up in New York from time to time."

Paul took out his notebook. "And how do you know that?"

"I've occasionally run across him in the club lobby the past few months."

"I'm surprised he'd have the courage to be seen there."

Vic was amused. "You're right, but you must understand our lobby's pretty much a public place. We don't have bouncers and I'm not inclined to take on that chore myself."

Paul, who had been far from a standout in his prep-school boxing classes, was quick to agree. He drifted as casually as he could to other subjects of no consequence, and finally came to the point that concerned him: "Tell me, Vic, have there been any significant changes in staff this year?"

Baines could think of none except the impending retirement of the associate club manager, Ross Lytton. (There was no club manager, Baines told Paul; the Search Committee that was to fill that position was "a little slow.") Lytton had reached age sixty-two and would receive a full pension. So far as Baines knew, it would be a perfectly friendly departure, although Lytton had told him on more than one occasion that he wished he could stay on. He'd been most cooperative in orienting his successor, so the change should go pretty smoothly. Baines personally would be sorry to see Lytton go. The poor fellow was strongly attached to the club, particularly since he'd attended the University for a couple of years, until family business reverses led him to drop out.

Paul asked him whether he was aware of any grievances that could account for the Friend's letters.

"They baffle me, Paul," Vic answered. "I think we run a first-class operation at the club. But we have a large membership, and it's quite a heterogeneous group. God only knows who may have gotten crosswise with whom."

By this time it was after six, Paul told Vic he had to get

back to the club. He and Alice had plans for dinner, followed by a Dietz and Schwartz musical at a little theater on Eighteenth Street. Baines asked the bartender for the bill. When it arrived, he subjected it to close scrutiny. His intent search for mathematical error reminded Paul of his friend Phil Randall, who performed a similar operation whenever they went to dinner together, an operation to which the Pryes had given the generic name "Randallizing a bill." When Vic Baines had finished his "Randallizing," he confirmed the total and suggested to Paul that they split it down the middle.

They paid and left the bar. Paul thanked Baines for his help and said he hoped they'd meet again at the club during his stay.

Alice's curiosity had been piqued by the events at the Alumni Club but she was not going to give up the rest of the summer to detection. Monday morning was business as usual for her. After Paul had left, she finished dressing and hailed a cab for her office at New York University's Institute of Fine Arts on Seventy-eighth Street.

The Institute of Fine Arts was housed in what had once been a private mansion, but in Alice's office the paraphernalia of scholarship had banished any traces of past elegance. Along two walls bookcases bulged with treatises and catalogs on nineteenth-century art and bound volumes of periodicals borrowed from the department's labyrinthine library. The lower bookshelves were tightly packed with boxes and carousels filled with slides for Alice's current lectures, and the path to her desk was impeded by utilitarian green metal file cabinets and a light-table for examining and masking slides.

Alice gave these familiar surroundings a glum Monday stare that was all they deserved. She sat down at her battered desk that had come with the office; she had never mastered the procedures for ordering a replacement and was not certain that such procedures existed. The desktop, unfortunately, was just as she'd left it on the day before the fire.

Drafts of proposed lectures and photocopied source materials fanned out in an apparently random arrangement whose secret was known only to her.

But on closer look she saw there was something else. Her office mail had been stacked in a few neat piles on the typewriter slide that projected from one edge of the desk. It must have been delivered by a temporary summer staffer, Alice thought. The regular deliveryman customarily shoved her mail under the door, leaving larger parcels (including, inevitably, occasional rejected manuscripts) in the hallway for her colleagues to examine.

It was only when Alice sifted through the last pile of her correspondence that she noticed an item out of the ordinary. It was a plain white envelope addressed to her in printed capitals. There was no stamp on the envelope, and her first thought was that it was a message from Nina Fox or one of her other faculty friends. But when she removed the letter she saw the seal of the Alumni Club. She read:

Dear Mrs. Prye,

I know you are a professor, but I thought that in your first days of widowhood even you would regard "Mrs." as a more appropriate title. Perhaps this is not correct. Still, the regrettable death of your husband has left us all at the Alumni Club in such a state of shock that I know I can count on your pardoning my confusion over how to address you under these strange circumstances.

Your husband (can I call him Professor Prye when you are Professor Prye as well and many would say the far more distinguished of the two?) had an inquiring mind. It was no doubt this quality (rather than a penchant for sensation and a lurking hostility) that spurred his notorious preoccupation with criminology. I for one do not believe that only aggressive people read about crime. The exception proves the rule.

The trouble is, I suppose, that it is one thing to spout off about old murders not everyone cares about and quite another to pose as an amateur investigator. It's rumored at the club that your husband recently overrated his competence as a detective and was doing some awkward sleuthing among our members. We don't like this kind of interference but of course forgave it in your husband, whom we have always regarded as well-meaning (though not necessarily the most practical man we've ever met).

It is bizarre, of course, that your husband, the perpetual student of crime, died a violent death. It was an accident, no two ways about that, but the appearances were ambiguous, just as Professor Prye (there, I've given him his title at last) would have wished had the tragedy only befallen someone else.

I hope you will find some comfort in these lines.

Sincerely,

A Friend from the Alumni Club

That does it, Alice decided at once. We've got to move back to the International.

CHAPTER 5

Their room was in an uproar. Paul's suits had been dumped in a tangle on his bed, and his ties and shirt sleeves trailed lifelessly from the top of the bureau. Alice's suitcases, strapped and locked, stood guard at the open door of the closet, now completely empty.

Alice sat on her bed, arms folded. In the best of circumstances, this was not a good sign.

"Where have you been?" Alice challenged him. "I've been calling Fayerweather Hall all day and they say you've not been to your office."

She handed him the Friend's new letter.

"Where'd you get this? I see that the envelope's not postmarked."

"It was delivered to my office. One of our summer messengers tells me she found it wedged under the front door at about eight this morning."

"Marvelous," Paul exulted after he read the letter. "I've had the feeling my inquiries were leading us nowhere, and yet somehow I've succeeded in getting under the Friend's skin."

"That's not my idea of success. You get under the Friend's skin, so she drops a flower pot on you and the late-news program talks about the perils of living in New York City; it's such a rosy prospect, no wonder you're looking forward to it."

Paul came over and sat down at the foot of her bed. "Alice, to quote the old coffee ads, you're overreacting. All the others who received these letters could just have easily feared for their lives, but everyone I've talked to seems to have treated them like bad jokes, and the Richardsons, who so far at least won't see me, seem to have gotten mad but no more than that."

Alice wasn't buying his assurances. "You're a better reader than that, Paul. The other letters didn't talk about violent death. That's probably why you had such a hard time figuring out whether they were death threats at all. This new letter doesn't leave much doubt on that score. And the talk about 'ambiguous appearances' makes it even worse. The Friend's warning how clever she can be about disguising a murder attempt."

Paul looked at the letter again before he answered. "I think you're getting so worked up over the nerve of this fellow's writing to you that you're missing the joke. I don't take the 'violent death' and 'ambiguous appearances' as any more than a satirical reference to my obsession with unsolved crimes. And that's the reason you don't find anything similar in the other letters." He looked closely at Alice to gauge the effect of his argument, and was cheered when she brightened a little.

"You know, Paul, I think there is something in what you say. The letter scared me so much I may have missed the point. Can you overreact from too many decafs?" She paused for a moment, beset by a new qualm. "It is puzzling, though. How would the Friend know so much about your interest in crime?"

"You remember our conversation on Friday when we were trying to figure out why Baker had invited us? You mentioned your Géricault lecture at the Alumni Club, but you had forgotten that I appeared on a program there myself. In fact, I think it was in the same year, 1983, if I'm not mistaken. By the way, Alice, your insistence on referring to the Friend as a female is not going unnoticed but I'm not going to quarrel with you about that until I know much more than I do now."

Alice ignored his concluding comment, since her mind had already darted elsewhere. "All right, I'll accept what you say. It's not surprising that the Friend could have picked up enough knowledge of your oddities to write the letter. But why did she write the letter, and why did she deliver it this morning?"

"I would guess that the Friend has somehow found out that we've been invited here and I've been asked to find out who he is. At the very least the letter's been written to express the Friend's displeasure. Remember what I told you about graphorrhea; he probably takes pen in hand at the slightest provocation."

"But isn't the Friend taking a dangerous course in surfacing with us so soon? After all, you've hardly begun your mission, and as of this morning you'd only met a handful of members. We'll put our sex war aside for the moment; aside from Rodney Baker and Victor Baines, let's try to recall together who we've talked to about the letters. Maybe that's the group where we'll track down the Friend."

Paul checked her enthusiasm. "I'm as anxious as you are to shrink the field of suspects, but I don't think we can do it as easily as you suggest. I'm sure there are many more people we haven't met who know about our assignment. In the first place, there's the Oversight Committee."

"The what?" Alice asked.

Paul forgot that he had not had a chance to bring her up-to-date on his day's conversations. "I guess I haven't told you about that yet, but we're going to have to hurry or we'll be late for the theater. They're doing *The Band Wagon*. What are we going to do about all this mess?" He swept an arm to survey the wreckage of the room.

Alice walked to the mirror to repair her cosmetics and threw her answer over her shoulder. "I guess we'll unpack when we get back to the room."

"That's a good idea," Paul said, "and when we do it, I'd like to discuss a re-allocation of the closet space." Without waiting for her response, he hurried downstairs to hail a cab.

On the way to the theater he told her about the Oversight Committee and the expulsion of the false Charlie Benson.

On Tuesday morning the Pryes tried out the club's continental breakfast. When they returned to their room the phone was ringing. It was Harry Fowler. His chairman, Bart Tucker, had done some testing of the Italian regionals last night and found that all the bottles sampled showed MSG above commercial levels.

Paul was irritated by Harry's cautious phrasing. "What do you mean, 'above commercial levels'? I would think you'd regard any MSG in your wines as too much."

"That would undoubtedly be true if we were talking about fine wines but, as I mentioned yesterday, it's not unprecedented for the bulk shippers to spruce up their products a bit. But what Bart found was that the quantities of MSG were so great that it's hard to believe any exporter who knew his business wouldn't realize he was overdoing things."

Alice went to the heart of the matter. "Are you trying to tell us, Harry, that these bottles have been tampered with? They have screw-on caps and are easier to open without anyone being the wiser."

"I don't see any value in speculating about that now. The important point is that we've ordered all the bottles removed from the cellar at once. I'm sorry to be brief, but my next patient's just arrived."

No sooner had the Pryes hung up than the phone rang again. Dave Emmerich was calling them from his office to report the lab findings on the ink.

"The chemistry department tells me this: First, that the ink in all three pens is the same, and second, that it matches the ink in both letters. They're not as confident about identifying the pen used. There is some evidence that the letter to Ms. Scroop might have been written by the pen you labeled No.

3. The point is worn and the ink flow is irregular. We see some similar effects in the Scroop letter. Where did you pick up that pen, Paul?"

"It is from the writing desk outside the club library."

"Anything new and exciting since we talked on Sunday?"

It might have been his usual optimism, but Paul thought that Emmerich was showing signs of getting hooked by the club mystery. As new lures, Paul told him about Charlie Benson and what they'd just learned about the wine.

When Emmerich hung up Alice began to fill her unorganized handbag in preparation for the day's excursions.

"And who is our MSG dispenser, Paul? Is it the Friend from the Alumni Club trying her hand at something new? And is it the same oddball who spoiled the new members' party by switching the cards?"

"I don't know," Paul said, "but it's possible that the Friend is at it again. Maybe the letter writing is starting to bore him, or perhaps it no longer satisfies him to torment his victims from a distance without being able to see their reactions."

Alice raised an objection. "Well, she can't be as sick of writing as all that; remember, it was only yesterday morning that I picked up my little billet-doux." She noticed that Paul had put his left index finger to his mouth, a good sign that he was more disturbed than his words had indicated. She therefore added, "Of course, I know you haven't forgotten our letter. What is it that's troubling you?"

"I'm not troubled really, I wouldn't call it that, but your guess that the Friend may be diversifying his attacks may be right on the button. I've had the same feeling over the weekend. It started with your bad wine and was confirmed by the squabble at the dining room table. It's begun to look like the Friend is inclined to experiment with new means of expressing hostility. There's nothing disturbing about that in itself, but I always tend to think that aggression merits a closer look when it turns from words to action."

When Alice left, Paul opened the club envelope he had deftly palmed when they came back to their room after breakfast. It had been slid vigorously under their door and came to rest near a wastebasket; fortunately Paul was able to retrieve it without Alice's noticing.

The envelope contained a telephone message: "Mr. Baker called. He will meet you at Squash Court 4 at 9:30 tonight. He'll bring rackets." The words were printed in capitals that rose from left to right.

Paul took out his spiral notebook and reached for the telephone. Rodney Baker answered. Rodney, who spoke more fluently over the phone than in person, asked him how the investigation was going.

"The people I've talked to have been pleasant enough, but I keep running into problems about official secrets. Maybe you can help declassify them."

Baker became more cautious. "For example?"

"I'd like to review the Admissions Committee files on rejections and expulsions."

Paul listened to Baker trying out different consonants. "That may be a pretty tall order, but I don't think you would find much of interest along those lines. You're talking about rare events."

"Rodney, you're the boss. This investigation is your idea and you can call it off at any time without insulting me. But I can't accomplish much, if 'rare events' are to be off limits. The Friend's letters, I hope, are themselves rare events."

There was silence at the other end of the line, so Paul continued. "Expulsions may not be all that common, and I would hope so for the sake of peace and tranquillity at the club, but we both know they happen. I've only been looking around for a few days and I couldn't help running headlong into the Benson business. Of course, Rodney, it didn't hurt at all that the scowling Miss Gustave gave us his room."

Continued silence. "Though, frankly, Rodney, if you're not playing games with me, you might just have stretched a point and told me about Benson at our first meeting."

Baker finally found his voice. "Is Benson a suspect?"

"How in the world would I know when there may be a lot more dubious characters in the Admissions Committee files you won't show me?"

"I haven't said no," Rodney drawled unconvincingly. "Let's say your request is under advisement. Can I do anything else for you?"

"What about the Richardsons?"

"I haven't given up on them yet, but I'm having trouble reaching them."

Paul had saved his favorite question for the last. "Rodney, who's on the Oversight Committee?"

"The Oversight Committee? There isn't any club committee by that name."

"Harry Fowler seems to think there is," Paul said, taking the receiver from his ear and looking at it with growing distaste.

"I think what Harry means is that certain of the members who are particularly concerned about the welfare of the club get together occasionally to talk about current issues in operations or planning."

"Would those members include you, for example?"

"From time to time, certainly, but they might include just about anyone who has something on his mind or something useful to contribute."

Paul decided that Rodney was not in a confessional mood, so he surrendered for the moment. "Thanks, Rodney, you've been a great help." He then added as if by afterthought, "Oh, by the way, Rodney, are you free by any chance tonight, say around nine-thirty?"

"As a matter of fact I have a community board meeting that will pin me down until late. What did you have in mind?"

"Alice and I were thinking of having some friends over to the club for drinks. Since you're paying our tab, I thought we should include you."

"Sorry about that," Baker said, "give me a rain check. I have to dash now. Good-bye."

Paul immediately dialed another number. Ben Tolliver's secretary answered. No, she said, Professor Tolliver couldn't meet him for lunch. He was in Europe on sabbatical, and had been there since May.

Good, Paul thought, I like old Tolliver, and besides, the Friend's letters aren't up to Ben's fine Elizabethan style.

Paul had no sooner hung up than his phone rang. He thought at first it was an aftershock of his decisive return of the receiver to its cradle, but a dreamy operator whispered, "John Richardson's office. Please hold."

Richardson! Was the man psychic? Baker wouldn't have had time to call him—unless they were together on the line. Paul's speculations were soon cut short by a suave voice.

"Professor Prye, this is John Richardson speaking."

"Yes, Mr. Richardson, how are you?"

"Quite well, thanks. I'm sorry to disturb you, but I have something on my mind I'd like to share with you."

"Yes?" Paul couldn't believe his ears. Was someone at the Alumni Club actually going to volunteer information?

"You may remember that some years back a famous adviser to a national administration recommended that a serious social problem be moderated by 'benign neglect.'"

"I remember very well," Paul said. "I think he took a lot of flak for his choice of words."

"That may be, but doesn't that always happen when someone goes public with a thought other people are too cowardly to express? I, too, happen to think that many social conflicts get worse if you stir them up too much. I've spent a goodly portion of my time in governmental matters and I can say, without immodesty, that I'm not without experience in these matters." There was a hint of a Georgia accent in his voice.

Paul began to see the light. "Do I take it that you think I may be stirring things up at the club that might be better left unstirred?"

Richardson laughed. "I couldn't have put it better. These anonymous letters, Professor Prye, aren't doing any real mischief. If we ignore them and don't give the writer the feeling he's getting to us, he'll soon find something better to do with his time. That's what happens with all hate mail."

"So you suggest I lay off," Paul said, continuing to offer blunt translations.

"I wouldn't be so presumptuous as to tell you what to do. I'm appealing to your judgment."

"Does it matter that Rodney Baker's judgment may be different than yours?"

There was a little silence. "Rodney is a prudent man, but this is a matter on which many thoughtful members disagree with him. I thought you'd want to know that."

Paul couldn't bring himself to utter the atrocious cliché "I hear you," but did not come up with a response that was much better. "Thank you very much for calling, Mr. Richardson; I'll consider what you've told me."

"That will be good enough, I'm confident of that." Richardson said. "You are a man of the world."

As a history professor, Paul had been called many things, but never that. He rather liked the way it sounded.

Alice didn't believe Paul when he concocted a story about a departmental meeting scheduled on a hurry-up basis for that evening, but she did not protest when he left her after dinner.

About nine-fifteen Paul took the stairs from the lobby to the eighth floor to avoid any chance of running into Alice, who never walked when she could ride. Most of the lights on the floor had been turned out and Paul couldn't locate the switches, but it was easy to find his way to Squash Court 4. It was the main court on which the big tournament matches were held. Glass partitions that formed two walls of the court permitted spectators to observe play from an L-shaped wooden grandstand. Paul sat on the bottom row of the grandstand and waited.

What if I'm wrong and someone really shows up? Paul thought. Incongruously, his first worry was of social embarrassment. He had been laughed off a few tennis courts when he was younger, but he hadn't the vaguest idea how to play squash.

He hunched his shoulders and squinted into the empty squash court, which was deeply hidden in shadow. It was imprudent of him to have come, he knew that. He was on unfamiliar territory here in the realm of club sports and was disoriented by the maze of passages that led from the ancillary courts to the principle corridor. Even in broad daylight his sense of direction was weak, and if an emergency awaited him now he would not know where danger might lie or how best to escape. Still he felt he was secure, for logic told him so.

He waited for a half hour, when logic was jolted; he heard the sound of footsteps approaching along the main hallway from the direction of the elevators. He turned partway only, determined in all events to shield any involuntary surprise, and observed a small man walking towards him in the gloom. The man walked slowly; he seemed to have seen Paul but did not hail him. When he skirted the grandstand and came into view, Paul recognized him at once. It was the red nose that gave the man away even in the darkness: the club's doorman was now transformed into its night watchman.

"Sir," he said, "I must ask you to leave this area. Under club rules, the squash courts close at nine."

When Paul, back in Room 759, confessed to Alice receipt of the telephone invitation and his visit to the squash court, she was far from pleased but too curious to withhold a question. "I don't get it. The Friend is getting clumsy; he knew you could find out the squash date wasn't real just by phoning Baker as you did."

"That was just the point, I think," said Paul, finishing his day's entries in his notebook. "He intended that I would know the message was from the Friend. The letter to you obviously didn't scare us off, so now it was my turn for a little game of 'wait in the dark.'"

CHAPTER 6

Wednesday was not a banner day for the Pryes. Alice's word processor had rebelled, and half a chapter had faded from its memory. Paul let her rail eloquently against the brutish machine, and against a French museum that was raising bureaucratic difficulties about reproduction rights. After she had calmed down under the soothing influence of the first afternoon vodka, he complained that he had not yet heard further from Baker and concluded:

"I'm sorry we unpacked Monday night. Maybe you were right; we ought to forget about the Friend and move out of this sanctum of the class of 1916."

Now it was Alice's turn to be stubborn. "And you don't even care to track down the joker who had the nerve to write your wife an upsetting letter and reneges on a promising squash pairing? Anyway, you can't quit effective immediately, because we're meeting Brian Kennedy for cocktails in about twenty minutes."

Paul stirred from his brooding. "You're right, I would have forgotten. Put on your face, I'll grab the rule book, and we'll be there with time to spare."

They found Brian waiting for them in the club barroom, a secret joke playing as always at the corners of his lips. It was not easy to get table service because of the staff's frantic preparations for the night's activities, so they agreed to sit at the bar. After they had ordered, Brian led off at a businesslike pace which the Pryes found surprising:

"I'll have to make this a quick one, I'm afraid, because I have to get home to change for Bessarabian Night."

"What on earth is Bessarabian Night?" Alice asked, ignoring the gentle kick Paul directed against her ankle to remind her that they had come to talk about the Friend.

Kennedy seemed to forget the time pressure he was under as he told them with obvious relish the story behind the evening's festivities.

"Bessarabian Night" had its origin in a humor piece that had appeared a few years earlier in the University's undergraduate newspaper, the *Oxblood*. The writer had satirized the social calendar of the Alumni Club which, the year round, was well stocked with such regular events as "Carnival in Old Vienna," "Sushi Fantasy," "Spring's Awakening," and, of course, the inevitable murder-mystery parties that Paul Prye thought had gone in and out of fashion four decades before. The columnist proposed, tongue in cheek, that a Bessarabian Night would be a worthy addition to the club's annual schedule. Written in the heavy-handed style for which the *Oxblood* was famous and heavily sprinkled with ethnic jokes about Kishinev and gypsies, the article seemed destined for a well-deserved obscurity. However, some of the new members of the Alumni Club, anxious to show that they could still take a joke after graduation, made the article their manifesto and formed a "club within a club," which they called the Bessarabians. Their monthly gatherings, planned with mock research to feature Bessarabian dress and cuisine, became so popular that the group's celebrations were transformed into the yearly event that the *Oxblood* had pretended to advocate. Bessarabian Night had immediately become the best attended of all the Alumni Club's festivities, surpassing even the Christmas party and often drawing close to five hundred members and guests.

"I hope you are coming," said Kennedy when he had

finished his sketch of the Bessarabians, of whom the Pryes suspected he was a charter member.

"Actually, we didn't know nonmembers could attend," Paul said unconvincingly, "and anyway, though you'd not guess it by our antics around here the last few days, we're actually both back to our regular work schedule."

"Early to rise," Alice summarized their plight with regret.

"Still, we mustn't spoil your evening," Paul said as he brought the conversation back to his sputtering investigation. "Let me just ask a few questions for the moment, and perhaps, if it's not inconvenient, we can get together again."

Kennedy nodded slightly to Paul and beamed at Alice. "That'll be fine, but I don't mean to rush you too much. What's up?"

"First, could you ask Melanie Ackerman to see me?"

"Consider it done; I'm expecting to see her tonight, a queen among the gypsies."

"Second, what can you tell me about Charlie Benson's expulsion?"

Kennedy fenced with him. "Suppose you begin by telling me what you know already, and I'll fill in if I can, though I should warn you I'm far from the most diligent member of the Admissions Committee."

Paul gave an abbreviated account of his own discoveries, of Vic Baines' disclosures regarding the fraudulent decoration of Room 759, and of Ralph Murray's grudging comments about the ejection of the fake Benson.

Kennedy was impressed or pretended to be so. "I think you already know as much as I do. If you want to know more about the details of the room renovation, Ross Lytton's your man, that is, if you can find him. As you may know, he's about to retire (I think it's effective July thirty-first) but he seems to be away more than he's here these days."

"Who would know where to reach him?"

"Probably Miss Gustave; have you met her?"

Alice grimaced. "We had the pleasure right off the bat."

"Okay," Paul said, following a mental checklist. "You don't seem to be such a keen devotee of Admissions and

House matters, but aren't you chairman of Athletics and Games?"

"Yes, indeed, that's the committee that keeps me slaving away. More the sports side, though. The chess and backgammon types don't need a lot of hand-holding."

"Just kibitzing, I suppose," Alice suggested.

Paul overlooked her remark and continued: "Have you had any unusual problems in club sports recently?"

Kennedy laughed. "You mean a sore loser who gets so mad he starts penning anonymous letters? I don't think anyone here takes squash all that seriously."

Alice was skeptical. "The painter Caravaggio killed his opponent after losing a tennis match, and if you give Paul half an opening, he'll tell you about a madman named Molineux who tried to poison a club athletic director for ordering the wrong brand of sports equipment."

Kennedy patted her shoulder affectionately and let his finger trail a respectable distance down her back. "I didn't know you folks were sports scholars. I won't say that athletes (with or without steroids) can't develop pretty big egos, but I think most of our members look on their squash as a form of exercise that's a good deal more sociable than jogging."

Kennedy paused for a moment's reflection. "Come to think of it, we have had one minor problem this summer. We haven't quite figured it out yet."

The Pryes perked up but waited patiently.

"I don't know whether you've visited the squash courts yet. As you leave the elevator on the eighth floor you face the attendant's desk and, above it, the blackboard where the pairings and court assignments are listed. In the last several weeks, there's been some confusion in the reservations; we've had four or even six players claiming a single court at the same hour."

"How do you make reservations?" Paul asked.

"You can call them in to the attendant and he'll post the reservation for you, or if you're in the club you can make your own entry on the blackboard."

"How long is the attendant on duty?"

"Supposedly from eight A.M. to six P.M., but the fellow we now have at the desk seems to have wanderlust."

"How does your committee account for the confusion?" Paul asked.

"We haven't put our finger on the answer. Some of the committee think the attendant is taking multiple phone reservations without paying attention to the blackboard."

Alice had a better idea. "Is it possible that someone's playing fast and loose with the chalk eraser?"

"Why would anyone want to do that?"

"Search me," Alice said, and then dropping her voice, added, "but then again I don't know why anyone would have wanted to rearrange the seating cards at a new members' dinner."

Kennedy downed the small remnant of his drink and Alice could not read his expression. At last he muttered, "I couldn't do much better with that question myself."

Paul let the matter rest, asking, "Are Richardson, Parry, and Corbett big for sports and games?"

"You sure wouldn't call any of them jocks. I think Corbett got an eye injury playing squash a few years back, and he seems to have given up the game. I don't think I've ever seen John or Vance on the courts."

"Just one last thing before we let you go," Paul said, looking apologetically at his watch. He drew a short breath he hoped was inaudible. "Are any of the three men on the Oversight Committee?"

Kennedy was not at all thrown off his stride and replied almost jovially, "You're really making rapid progress in your initiation into club politics. I congratulate you both. I would guess that John Richardson must be a member, but I wouldn't be sure about Vance and even less so about Miles. The problem is that the oversight honchos aren't a formal committee and they keep their business pretty private. They sure don't confide in me. Despite the committee assignments the club throws my way, I'm not exactly an insider here. I'm the guy who can be counted on to handle a few pledge cards or to plan a social evening. I guess you could say I'm one of the club's 'balloon blowers.'"

"Does Mrs. Kennedy also help with the social events?" Alice asked with a trace of emphasis.

"There hasn't been a Mrs. Kennedy in my family since my mother died," Brian said and, with a quick handshake for Paul and another pat for Alice, he left them at the bar.

"What do you make of our friend?" Paul asked when he'd passed from earshot.

"He's missed his calling; I think he'd make a great masseur."

Alice was a passionate people watcher; this evening she had prevailed on Paul to put off their dinner reservation a little so that she could observe the entries of the Alumni Bessarabians. She claimed a couch that faced the front door of the club so that they would miss very little of the pageantry. At first she was a little disappointed, because many of the early arrivals, including some of the club dignitaries she had met on Saturday night, were not in Balkan costume. She nodded disapprovingly at the pinstripes of the fashion plate Ralph Murray and paunchy Victor Baines but then her eyes shot back to the door, which opened to admit a phalanx of oriental Bessarabians with painted Mikado eyes and Zouave trousers.

"Who are they supposed to be?" Alice whispered.

"Obviously some of Bessarabia's conquerors," Paul said, falling easily into historical speculation, "but I suppose that if you're not one of the club's elite you can't tell a Turk from a Tartar without a program."

Alice was no longer listening, because a bevy of the gypsy women Brian Kennedy had promised them were arriving. Among their ranks Melanie Ackerman laughed raucously. She wore by far the reddest Romany dress and a rose in her hair, but Saturday night's black patent leather bag was slung from her shoulder. "Where has Tom gone to?" she called, and the gypsies turned back towards the door in time to

witness the solo entrance of a Saint Michael with an attached
halo that added to his already considerable height.

"Great taste," Alice murmured to Paul, "if Simmons is so
persuaded of his innocence, why can't he let anyone forget
his damn trial for a minute?"

"Maybe his prison book is going into another edition,"
Paul suggested, involuntarily mindful of his own small
academic printings.

Brian Kennedy waved to the Pryes as he walked past them
to Bainesgate and the Great Hall. He and a statuesque
brunette by his side were matched in red-peaked fur hats,
golden sandals with upturned toes, and fur-trimmed robes of
blue and gold to which they had pasted large decals reading
"Polovtsian Man" and "Polovtsian Maiden."

Paul seemed taken with the Bessarabians, so Alice decided
to press her luck. "We still have a few minutes before dinner;
can we take a peek at the Hall?" Hearing no objection, she
offered him her arm and they followed the newest contingent
of Bessarabians trooping to the public rooms.

The Hall had been spectacularly disguised by the club staff
and by the membership's dedicated workhorses whom Brian
Kennedy had called the "balloon blowers." The gallery was
hung with bunting in the traditional blue, yellow, and red
tricolor of Romania. The same colors shone down from
spotlights fixed halfway up the walls; they also predominated
in massive flower arrangements in the far corners of the Hall
and in the bouquets and napkins on the dining tables that
filled the main floor to overflowing and sprawled along the
east gallery above.

"I'm glad we didn't come," Alice said, "they would have
'skyed' us." Her pet peeve was chic benefit dinners held in
multi-level courthouses or utility buildings. If you were
placed on the top tier, your beef arrived cold and the guest
celebrity never arrived at all.

The Pryes observed that each place setting was furnished
with a stout unlighted candle in a clear glass votive recepta-
cle. Remembering the New Members' Party, they suspected
that the candles were not there for romance but to supply

auxiliary illumination in the event of another short circuit in the air-conditioning system.

A little embarrassed by their uninvited status and non-Balkan attire, Alice and Paul ventured a modest distance farther into the Great Hall to admire the decoration of the club's monumental fireplace. Above the mantelpiece they looked in vain for the University's seal, incised with its famous slogan, *Integer Vitae*. For the evening this emblem was covered by two banners with crudely drawn portraits of Romanian rulers that hung down from the railing of the gallery and billowed as the glass entrance doors from the lobby opened to admit new guests. The monarch at the left was unfamiliar to the Pryes but the artist had informed them by a brilliant red legend that he was Prince Basarab I, the fourteenth-century Romanian hero who had given his name to Bessarabia. Basarab's companion needed no introduction to the Pryes. His bulging black eyes under pencil-thin high arched brows, his prominent nose drooping down across a bushy mustache, and the familiar eight-pointed star with enclosed lozenge set in his dotted hatband, announced him to be Vlad the Impaler, the infamous Wallachian original of Dracula. Scanning the growing throng of costumed Bessarabians, the Pryes counted at least a half dozen pallid imitations of Vlad, including Rodney Baker. They compensated for melting cosmetics and semi-detached mustaches by carrying wooden stakes that represented Vlad's dreaded weapon. "They're not very convincing," Alice said, "I guess the club has more WASPs than Wallachians. Still, I *do* like their stakes. If this were one of Agatha Christie's parties, she could do wonders with the stakes."

Paul, dinner forgotten for a while, continued to survey the costumes. "Alice, I win the door prize; I've finally spotted Basarab himself." He pointed to one of the bars that had been set up below the overhang of the east gallery, where a gaunt, silver-haired man in princely garb was handing a tulip glass of champagne to a woman. Also dressed in royal robes, she smiled up at him without lipstick, her shoulder-length gray hair bobbing slightly as she accepted the drink.

Alice looked more closely at the couple, then pulled at Paul's sleeve. "You've done better than you think, you've finally located the Richardsons. Don't you remember him from the Senate hearings?"

"I believe you're right. Interesting, isn't it, that he's so obviously at home here in the robes of Basarab the Great."

"He's the monarch," agreed Alice, "no doubt about that, and our friend Rodney Baker's only one of the Vlads."

The Pryes were glad that they were at length able to tear themselves away from Bessarabian Night, for the cassoulet that they ordered at the bistro was first-rate. They lingered over brandy, because the restaurant was staffed and frequented by the theater crowd and they liked to wait to see the chorus lines gather for drinks after eleven. Tonight, though, Paul was distracted. He had taken one of the giant crayons that served as a centerpiece and was scrawling on the tablecloth. Alice could see that he had not been stricken with sudden artistic fervor but was arranging and rearranging lists of people. Among them she could read upside down the names of some of the club members they had met, but others were unfamiliar. She said nothing and let him write on.

They returned to the club and were in bed by about midnight. Paul's sleep was troubled. He thought he saw flashing red lights and heard the wailing of sirens. Alice, who once she hit the pillow recovered the conscience of a newborn baby, slept dreamlessly.

CHAPTER 7

It was Alice who told Paul about Melanie's death. She had intended to leave for Riverdale early Thursday morning to check on the painters. When she left the elevator, however, she was stunned to find the Great Hall swarming with police. From a young man at the front desk she received only a sketchy account of what had happened, but it was enough to send Alice back to her room to wake up Paul.

Together they heard the details on the radio:

> Early this morning a woman fell to her death from the high balcony of midtown's prestigious Alumni Club.
>
> The victim was Mrs. Lester Ackerman, 35, a club member.
>
> Details on the accident are scanty. Last night the club held its summer costume party. Sometime after midnight, the electricity at the club shorted out but the party continued by candlelight. About an hour later, Melanie Ackerman fell from the two-story gallery that overlooks the main hall where the dinner was held. She died immediately of multiple fractures of her skull and spine.
>
> The club's president, in Martha's Vineyard on vacation, deplored Mrs. Ackerman's death as "the most

tragic accident in the history of the Alumni Club."
Lester Ackerman, the victim's husband, reacted with
anger to questions about his wife's death. Mr. Ackerman, a retired lawyer, did not attend the party. He said
that there is altogether too much drinking at the club's
events and that "things tend to get out of hand." He
added that "the club's macho poet laureate has popular-
ized a damn foolish game he calls 'skywalking.' The
members drink until they're half blind, then walk or
slide along the mahogany railing of the gallery. The club
keeps the rail so highly polished it's nothing short of an
'attractive nuisance.'"

Mr. Ackerman did not state whether his wife had ever
tried "skywalking" or whether anyone had seen her
doing so before her death. Club officials were silent on
the subject. Some members confirmed that the "poet
laureate" to whom Ackerman had referred is Jack
Feldman, who recently gained new notoriety in connection with his support for the parole of convicted wife-
murderer Thomas Simmons.

The Medical Examiner is expected to rule formally on
the cause of Mrs. Ackerman's death in a day or two.

When the report was finished, Alice was disappointed that
Paul had no immediate reaction. "I must say, you don't seem
very excited. What do you think?"

Paul's thoughts seemed elsewhere, as he said quietly, "I
think we better call Baker for more details; I'll shower and be
dressed in a few minutes."

Paul could try to sound as blasé as he liked but he wasn't
fooling Alice. She changed from her home-repair pantsuit
look into an olive dress Paul particularly liked and waited for
him.

At last Paul emerged from the bathroom. "The olive dress,
just the inconspicuous thing a detective's wife should wear.
Where did we find it—Athens, I think. Or maybe we found
olives in Athens and the dress elsewhere." He kissed her and,
after dressing, called Baker. Rod said he'd come right over,
so the Pryes went downstairs to look around.

They found that their look was tightly circumscribed.
Entry to the Great Hall was barred by an oxblood velvet rope
that sagged between two metal stanchions. Alice was reminded fleetingly of many similar barriers that had blocked
their entrance to theaters at which her husband had insisted
on arriving before the cast and stage crew.

Paul, craning his neck through the archway, looked to the
left where a tarpaulin broke the rich dark surface of the
carpet. He said, as much to himself as to Alice, "That's where
the body must have fallen. Strange that it should have been
there."

Alice ignored his last comment because her mind was still
on the unsightly canvas. "Why do you suppose they've
thrown it there? Is it to spare us the unpleasant sight of
bloodstains, or do you suppose the homicide squad has
chalked the outline of the body the way they do on television?" When Paul didn't answer, she picked up his last
words. "Why do you say it's odd that the body should have
fallen there?"

"I seem to remember that there were additional tables set
up along the eastern wing of the gallery, but Melanie seems
to have fallen from the opposite side." He bent forward again
to verify the position of the tarpaulin. "In fact, she must have
fallen from a point near the library, where there's a writing
desk from which I filched one of the pens. Why do you
suppose she would have strayed so far from the other
diners?"

"Skywalking?" Alice suggested.

Paul didn't think so. "I doubt whether even Jack Feldman
would advocate skywalking in the dark, except in some of
his more extravagant poems."

As if they had eyes in the back of their heads, they both
turned around in time to see Rodney Baker advancing
towards them through the grillroom. They shook hands and
headed off together towards the lounge.

"Dreadful business, that, just dreadful." That was about all
they could get Rodney to say until they had ordered a second
round of drinks.

"But how could it have happened, Rodney?" Alice asked, knowing that the subject of Melanie's death had remained on everyone's minds and needed no reintroduction.

"I just don't know, that's the worst of it; you see, Carla and I left quite early." Carla was Rodney's wife, whom the Pryes knew only slightly.

"Do you know who Melanie came with?" Paul asked. "The report said that Lester wasn't here."

"That's right. I'm not sure that Melanie came with anybody, really." The "really" spoke volumes of evasion.

"Paul and I saw her come in. She seemed to arrive about the same time as Tom Simmons."

"That could be," Rodney conceded after a pause. "The fact is, they sat together at dinner. And Carla and I completed the table."

"Were the seating arrangements made in advance?" Paul asked.

"Oh yes, the Bessarabians, for all their clowning, are a very formal bunch. I did ask, however, that Simmons be put at our table. I felt very bad about the mess–up we had with the place cards on the new members' night."

"Where was your table?" Paul asked.

"It was up on the east gallery. Some of us who are active at the club like to take some of those tables, because, as you can imagine, there is a good deal of grumbling among the members when they get put up there. You'd think it was Siberia."

"You mean, instead of Bessarabia." Alice followed up her words with a smile that was completely wasted.

"I suppose I'll sound facetious," Paul said, "if I ask you where you were when the lights went out."

"Not at all. In fact, Carla and I were well on our way home."

"Did anyone see Melanie fall?"

"Not so far as we've been able to tell."

"Who was the last person to see her on the gallery?"

"We can't even say that for sure. Tom Simmons seems to

have lost track of her a lot earlier. He tends to table-hop quite a bit; we learned that very early in the evening."

"Did he see her last before or after the power failure?"

Rodney considered the question carefully. "I don't believe that he is even sure of that, but I don't think the party was affected that much when the lights went out. The Bessarabians had been smart enough to provide candles at the tables."

"But there weren't any candles on the west gallery, were there?" Alice asked.

Rodney shook his head. "No, I don't believe so; I think you're right about that."

"Is there any truth in this skywalking business?" Paul watched Rodney search for the right line to take.

"Absolutely none, so far as I'm aware. But if there were any such shenanigans, Lester'd be the last one to know; he's almost never around the club." After a pause Baker appeared to moderate the strength of his assurances. "Nobody who was here last night has reported any inappropriate behavior or any overindulgence at the bars."

Paul let the conversation flag for a while and then asked with an abruptness that he had not intended: "Where does Melanie Ackerman's death leave the assignment you've given me? Do I drop my search for the Friend?"

Far from being offended by what Paul feared had been an insensitive question so soon after the accident, Rodney replied without hesitation. "Of course I would like you to continue your inquiries. It may be appropriate to low-key the investigation while life settles down to normal again. But I don't have to give you lessons in tact, you've done just fine so far and I haven't heard a single complaint. And the House Committee chairman seems pleased."

"That's good. By the way, how are you doing with the Richardsons?"

"Keep the faith," Rodney replied as he signed their bar check and rose to leave them. "He won't hold out forever, I feel sure of that. In the meantime, I have one bit of good news. Ralph Murray and his colleagues on the Admissions Committee have agreed to let you look at their files."

"Marvelous. When did you hear from them?"

"Ralph called me this morning; you must have been most persuasive."

"If so, let's try a little bit more persuasion. Since Victor Baines is happy with my discretion, do you think you could prevail on him to show me the House Committee records on the renovation of our room?"

"I don't see why not."

The Pryes had dinner that night in the sparsely populated club dining room. When the waiter had taken their order, Alice leaned across the table and asked, "Well, where do we go from here?"

Paul pretended not to understand. "We both heard what Baker said, and I've long been convinced that—despite John Richardson's warning—he must speak in some fashion for the club. I'm to continue the search for the poison penman but at a moderate pace until the furor over Melanie Ackerman calms down."

"Come off it Paul, I wasn't wed yesterday. You don't expect me to believe you think Melanie's death was a coincidence. Even Baker doesn't buy that. Given his limited trustee's vocabulary, he couldn't have made that plainer."

"He is worried, I'll grant you that," Paul said.

"So now your polite little inquiry has suddenly turned into a homicide investigation and your brain is teeming with thoughts you're not generous enough to share. Okay, I'm used to that, so I'll give you some ideas of my own."

"Straight from Agatha Christie, as usual," Paul predicted with a sigh. "Well, I'm listening."

Alice was satisfied with his submission. "Theory One. The Friend's letters were death threats after all. He's finally started putting his malice into action. It all fits your poison-pen lecture so well. Words were the first expression of his hostility, but he's played around with annoying pranks as well—messing up the place cards, confusing the squash pairings, even tampering with the wine. Now he's down to serious business and he's started to strike at the lives of his enemies."

"And who are his enemies?"

Alice's impatience was temporarily assuaged by the arrival of their shrimp cocktails.

"Why, we agreed on that long ago, it's the targets of his condolence notes."

"Is that the recipients or the men whose deaths he laments?"

"Either or both, please stop distracting me with details. In any event, we've heard that he's recently sent a condolence note to Melanie Ackerman. We don't know what it said but it was nasty enough to upset her, judging from what you were told by Aileen Scroop. This morning the Friend picked Melanie as his first victim. Maybe he planned it that way, knowing the trouble the club's been having with its lights and hoping he'd find her somewhere in the dark. Somewhere, did I say? Perhaps he did better than that and had a look in advance at the seating chart, which placed her conveniently high up on the gallery."

"Fascinating," Paul said in a tribute that was not entirely ironic. "But tell me this: If the Friend is starting to pick off his letter targets one by one, why is he starting in reverse? I think the Corbett-Scroop letter was first."

"I haven't quite worked that out yet," Alice said modestly, "but, Paul, aren't you being a bit forgetful? It isn't quite in reverse, you know; the most recent letter we know of came to me—unless, of course, we count your bogus squash invitation." Without giving him a chance to retrieve his words, she went on: "There's no need to reassure me about our safety, you've already done that to my satisfaction, and besides, this is where Agatha Christie comes to our aid. You see, I don't believe in my first theory at all, I've just spun it out for your entertainment. Agatha teaches us that our first thought is always backwards, and so I launch into Theory Two. The Friend is not a murderer, she is this morning's victim. You know I've suspected a woman from the start, and despite your incessant snooping you haven't shown me yet a better candidate than the late Melanie Ackerman. We've been taught to say nothing but good of the dead, but can't I get you to confess she had enough guile and aggression to match your personality portrait of anonymous letter writers?

"And if she was the Friend, don't some of the objections vanish? The murderer did not, to use your phrase, work in reverse. In fact, Melanie Ackerman never received a poison-pen letter at all, or if she did, she wrote it to herself, like that horrible French woman you mentioned, Marie What's-her-face. But somehow one of her real victims was on to her, was awfully riled up. He arranged to meet her on the gallery last night and pushed her over. I'm willing to bet you've seen the last of the anonymous letters, and that is my real reason for not rushing upstairs to pack. That and the delicious filet mignon which is still to come. Impressed?"

"Absolutely, it's an open-and-shut case. In fact, there's really nothing more to be said; I really should cancel Friday's appointment with Dave Emmerich." He grinned at Alice's startled look.

"We're meeting Dave Friday?"

"Right. It's lunch here at twelve, if Manet will leave you free for an hour or so."

"What are we going to talk to Dave about?"

Paul replied nonchalantly as he attacked his filet. "You're getting just like Agatha Christie, you've turned things backwards again. You see, it's Dave who wants to talk to us. He's seen the autopsy report."

"What does it say?"

"I don't know, he didn't seem to want to say over the phone, but he did tell me he's assigned himself to look into the Ackerman case."

Dave Emmerich was all business when he met the Pryes on Friday. His usual good-natured gibes at Paul's amateurism, which had set the tone of their Sunday conversation in SoHo, were packed away for another day.

"What's the Medical Examiner's ruling?" Paul asked. "We haven't seen anything in the papers yet."

Emmerich scowled.

"And I'm afraid you aren't going to for some time. I thought we might have something pretty definitive by now; he's studied the autopsy report but he's not prepared to make a decision yet."

"And what does the autopsy find?"

Dave rubbed his temple in what looked to Paul like feigned deliberation.

"Can I trust you two? Probably not, so my only hope is that nothing that's happening in the real world will hold your interest for long. So here are my secrets." He reached into his breast pocket and withdrew a Xerox copy of a typed report which he unfolded and held for a moment in his lap, a tantalizing distance from the myopic Pryes. Before he could, as he intended, slide the report face down beside his plate, he felt a heavy hand on his shoulder. Looking up, he was puzzled to see the stern face of the maître d'.

The incongruity of the situation was more than the Pryes could take with straight faces. Alice didn't laugh outright but the iced tea that she held to her lips rattled. "Don't worry, Dave," Paul said, "you're not under citizen's arrest. You're just being confronted with one of the club's many rules. We're supposed to avoid the public display of business papers." The maître d' nodded approvingly and walked away.

"Serves me right, too," Emmerich replied, folding the report and putting it back in his pocket. "I never should have shown it to you anyway. I probably put off my dishonorable discharge from the force for a year or two. Still, I am willing to tell you a little bit about the autopsy results if you don't scream them all over Fifth Avenue."

"We're listening," Paul said, encouraging him. "You're not going to tell us that it wasn't the fall that killed her."

"That fall would have killed anybody. But that's not the problem; it's that the fall doesn't seem to account for what we discovered in the body or what we don't see."

Paul's eyes glistened. "I get it: absence of contrecoup."

"Exactly."

Alice was exasperated. "Do you fellows mind translating for an art historian?"

Paul gestured to Emmerich to do the honors.

"Let's see how well I remember my forensics. Head injuries that are suffered in a fall occur, of course, when the moving head strikes a fixed object. The injury to the brain occurs not only at the point of impact (what the lab boys call the coup injury) but also, and often more dramatically, directly opposite the point of impact, this is the so-called contrecoup injury; I don't have to tell a French scholar this means counterblow. The contrecoup results from a continuing inertial movement of the brain inside the skull which causes a portion of the brain opposite the point of impact to pull away and expand with force back against the skull."

"Fascinating," Alice said, "and how did all these wonders work themselves out in the case of poor Melanie?"

"That's what has me worrying. You see, the autopsy showed that Mrs. Ackerman had severe contusions at her hairline on the right side and a depressed skull fracture on the same side where the skull was pushed into the brain. Nevertheless, there is no sign of a contrecoup injury to the brain opposite the skull fracture. The absence of a contrecoup suggests that her head was stationary when it was struck with a moving object."

Paul was racing far ahead in his conjectures. "What position was Melanie in when she was found on the floor?"

Emmerich shook his head. "That's just it, I wish we knew. I've heard about every version you could imagine except that she was standing upright. A flock of people rushed to her and tried every revival device that's in the books, and then some. We have no idea how she landed, but the dreadful injury to her right shoulder suggests that she fell on her side."

Paul seemed glad to turn away from her injuries. "Did you find her shoulder bag?"

"Yes, it must have swung loose in the fall but we picked it up on the carpet not far from the body."

"Did you inspect it?"

Emmerich looked offended. "Of course, we looked into it. We've read the same police procedurals you have, you know."

"I'm sure you have. And what did you find?"

"Nothing out of the ordinary: a wallet, key ring, cosmetics bag, contact-lens case, that kind of thing. Were you expecting anything else?"

"Not really," Paul said vaguely.

Emmerich's investigative technique was far from subtle. By Saturday everyone Paul spoke to at the club knew that Dave was nosing around and wasn't completely satisfied that Lester Ackerman had figured out how his wife had died. Maybe Dave's ham-fisted style was a blessing because Paul found that the club members were much more willing to cooperate with his own inquiry. Of course, Emmerich might have had nothing to do with the change of attitude. Perhaps it was Rodney, Vic Baines, Richardson, or the whole Oversight Committee, for all Paul could tell, who had put out the word that the time for stonewalling was past.

Whatever the reason, Paul found that Saturday was a very productive day. His first phone call had been to Brian Kennedy, who by his own words had been deep into Bessarabian party planning. Brian was able to bring him a copy of the party seating chart. Even Paul's cursory glance confirmed Baker's statement that many club officials had made the ultimate sacrifice of accepting seating in the gallery. It seemed to Paul, however, that this custom smacked as much of snobbery as of noblesse oblige. The groundlings could raise their eyes to the gallery for a quick lesson in who's who at the Alumni Club.

Without being asked, Brian had his own thoughts to offer on Melanie's death: "Lester's comments are a lot of crap. We know that and he knows it as well as anybody. He's never liked the club and feels like a fish out of water here. He's not a University graduate, you know. If you'd ever met him I wouldn't have to tell you that. I don't know why he came up with his asinine skywalking routine. There was a party a few years ago—I think it was Bessarabian Night—when Jack Feldman, to scare the hell out of everybody, pretended he was going to walk on the railing. He was easily restrained because he had no intention of doing anything of the sort. But this is the kind of thing that passes into club folklore, and maybe Lester was there that night, I don't remember.

"The real facts are much sadder. For all her bravado, Melanie Ackerman was very insecure socially and it was never plainer than at the big club functions. The only way she could get through these affairs was to drink up a storm. That's exactly what she was doing Wednesday night. But I think she was worse off than I'd ever seen her."

"Why do you think that was?" Paul asked.

"As a matter of fact, she told me she had received one of these condolence letters you're chasing after, and she was extremely upset."

"I wonder why it affected her that way? A number of other people at the club have received these letters, as you know. None of them was thrilled but Melanie seems somehow to have overreacted."

Kennedy didn't think so. "That was my first impression when she told me what was bothering her and I told her so. It didn't take me long to change my mind. You see, her note was different. The writer was condoling with Melanie on her own coming death."

"Of illness?" Paul asked.

"That's just the point, the letter was very vague as to how Melanie would die. That's just what made her feel so threatened. There was something else that was bugging her too."

Paul prompted him. "Did she tell you?"

"No, she didn't, and she made it pretty clear she wouldn't welcome my asking."

Paul thought of his long-standing debate with Alice. "Did she indicate at least whether the note was from a man or a woman?"

"Not even that. But she told me the writer was at the party and that she was going to have it out with the idiot before the night was out. She sounded braver than she was, I think. That's why she was fortifying herself with champagne. When I last saw her around midnight she was feeling no pain. She certainly had no business walking along a dark gallery unescorted."

"So you think she just didn't know where she was going and toppled over the railing?"

"Possibly, but I've got a better idea that I've already mentioned to Lieutenant Emmerich, so I might as well try it on you as well. Suppose she was looking down from the gallery and spotted—or thought she spotted—her letter writer. She leans over the balcony to take a better look, to call his attention, to curse him, who knows, and she falls."

"How could she see anyone down there in the darkness?"

"Oh, it wasn't as dark as all that. The power failure hardly came as a big surprise, it's almost a regular feature of our summer events at the club. There were candles burning at all the tables, and then everybody who was there, or at least everyone who was in the know, had come equipped."

"Equipped?" Paul asked.

"Of course," said Kennedy, "most of us had flashlights."

It was midmorning when Paul went upstairs to his room for a closer look at the seating chart. Alice had left and her parting message was propped against his night-table lamp: "P: I'm off to find a skirt and jacket to match that new blouse you adore. I leave the investigation in your capable hands. A. P.S. Don't trust Kennedy. He can't resist attractive women."

Paul was about to settle down with the seating chart when he noticed that the red message light on the phone was flashing. He called the desk and found that he had messages from Victor Baines and Ralph Murray. Baker must really be rallying the troops, Paul thought; they're stumbling over each other to offer assistance. Baines had called a few minutes before Murray, so Paul, in his methodical style, called him first. Vic was polite but wasted no time in proceeding to business.

"I got a call from Rodney Baker last evening. He told me that you'd like to see the House Committee files on the renovation of the 1916 room. You really could have asked me yourself. I don't think the committee would have any objection to that. Could you meet me at the bank around noon?"

Paul was puzzled. "The bank?"

"Yes, the Midtown National branch, right next door to the club. You enter right through the lobby."

"Yes, I've noticed, of course, but I'm surprised they're open on Saturday."

"They're not open for bank business, but the offices are open and they let us use their conference rooms. When you walk through the connecting door, you'll find the safe depository on your left; turn right and the first door to the left is Conference Room A. I will meet you there, and by the way, Ralph Murray will also be there. I understand that he's bringing some Admissions Committee files you've asked for."

"Thanks, Victor. I'll see you at noon."

Paul hung up and immediately called Ralph Murray. Ralph was distinctly formal; ice seemed to form on his every word. "As I think you predicted when we met for lunch, Baker has asked us to show you some of our recent files. We will agree because we have high regard for his judgment and also expect to be able to rely on your discretion. Can you meet me at Midtown National at noon?" He was about to give detailed directions when Paul interrupted to tell him that he had already received instructions from Victor Baines.

The mention of Baines did not exactly introduce a warming trend. "Yes, Rodney told me that Baines would be there."

If Paul could trust his social antennae, he suspected that there was no love lost between Murray and Baines. Yet it was hard to tell. Some people tended to be gruff over the telephone, and Murray in any event had not liked having his arm twisted regarding the delivery of his files.

Perhaps Murray was concerned about the impression he was making, for he felt compelled to add a brief explanation. "Baines and I are attending a club meeting for the afternoon anyway, so when he heard I was going to arrange to see you he thought we might as well both deliver our files at the same time. Our meeting should be over about five. Do you think that will give you enough time?"

Dumb question, Paul thought. How do I know what they're going to give me? But with his usual diplomacy he responded, "I'm sure it will be more than enough time."

Paul arrived at the conference room a little before noon. It was a small room, with an oval table accommodating eight persons. Neither Murray nor Baines was there, so Paul deposited his briefcase on the table and walked back into the corridor. His attention was attracted by the sound of voices farther down the hallway. He looked to his left and saw a group of men gathered at the open door of another conference room. Among them he recognized Miles Corbett talking to John Richardson, whose bearing seemed every bit as commanding as when he had been costumed as Basarab the Great.

After a few minutes the group disappeared into the other conference room. Paul, with nothing left to occupy his attention, turned back to enter room A. As he did so he saw Baines and Murray approaching from his right. Each of them was carrying a disappointingly slim file.

"Hello, Paul," Baines called from a distance, but Murray remained silent, training his eyes at the far end of the corridor. Paul, playing the host, ushered them into the conference room and waited patiently for them to entrust their records to him. Baines tossed his manila file onto the table and filled his meerschaum. "Well, there it is, the story of our committee's biggest blunder, whatever value it may have to you. I fear, though, it won't add much to what you already know."

Ralph Murray was not as easily parted from his committee's dossier. He clutched under his left arm a red gusseted file
that held the Admissions Committee's current records while
he swore Paul to secrecy. "I give you these with considerable
reluctance, as you know, and expect that nothing you learn
will go outside club walls."

Paul couldn't help thinking they were outside club walls
already but he nodded soberly. Then, gathering courage, he
decided to venture a little beyond what they might regard as
an outsider's privileges.

"It was terrible news about Mrs. Ackerman's death," he
said, addressing his words to neither of them in particular.

It was Baines who responded. "It was a tragic death, and,
as our president Jim Preswick said, a tremendous shock to
the club as well. It doesn't make things any easier when we
read what Mr. Ackerman has said. We run a very safe
clubhouse, I can assure you of that." Then, remembering the
file he was lending to Paul, he added, "Parenthetically, I
should acknowledge that you may not think the House
Committee deserves high marks on room decoration, Paul,
but the house is safe and sound."

Paul's eyes slid over in Ralph Murray's direction. Murray
didn't like Baines much, that now seemed clear, and he had
shown no signs of being wild about Paul, but he did observe
the proprieties. At last he said, "Melanie Ackerman will be
missed. She was a very popular member." Paul thought
he leaned a little on the word "popular" and wondered
whether he was freighting it with some special meaning. He
waited a little but nobody had anything more to say about
Melanie. Instead, Baines and Murray, their duty done, left
Paul alone with their files, promising to return at five. If he
finished earlier he could leave them in the room. The door
would automatically lock and the bank had given them the
key.

When they stepped back into the corridor they turned left
in the direction of the room where Richardson and the others
were meeting.

Paul closed the door of Conference Room A and prepared

for his afternoon's work. He attacked the Admissions Committee files first. The slimness of the folder was easily explained: Murray had not delivered any raw records but had included statistics on applications, admissions, and expulsions for the past year and short summaries of the careers and University ties of candidates. The limitations of the material were self-evident. For example, the name of Ben Tolliver was nowhere to be found. Presumably unsuccessful candidates became nonpersons and vanished from the records of the club, just as disgraced Russian politicians evaporated from the pages of the Great Soviet Encyclopedia. Still, the statistical summary told a suggestive tale.

In the past year there had been 127 applications filed and 115 admitted to membership. If it was assumed that some applications had been withdrawn because of business moves or unexpected financial hardship, the number of unsuccessful candidacies must have been small indeed. As Paul compared the statistics with prior years, he found that the size of the club had steadily increased and that the gap between applications and admissions had continuously narrowed.

He focused next on the expulsion records. In the past twelve months the club had terminated fifteen memberships. In fourteen cases the stated reason was nonpayment of dues, and most of the members involved were unsurprisingly nonresidents who may have found that their use of club facilities had become too infrequent to justify continued contributions. One name stood out in the list: Charles Benson IV. The word "sic" had been placed in parenthesis after his name and the ground of expulsion was stated to be "insufficient credentials." The effective date of termination of Benson's membership privileges was March 25 of the current year.

It was easy for Paul to skim through the House Committee folder. There were duplicates of invoices from furniture suppliers that he quickly put aside, wondering, though, whether that furniture could really be new; a series of memoranda from Ross Lytton to Baines furnishing estimates, reporting progress, complaining of delay, urgently requesting instructions. There was disappointingly little about "Charlie Benson"; Paul hardly glanced at the Xerox copies of the photographs proposed for Room 759's walls. One item, though, he noted for mention to Emmerich: a brief transmittal letter to Lytton written by Benson in longhand and closed with a flamboyant signature. The file contained no reference to Benson's imposture or its discovery.

CHAPTER 8

The man who met him when the elevator door opened on a high floor of an eastside apartment building did not tally with Paul's limited notions of a complaisant husband. Lester Ackerman looked like a recently retired middleweight still in fighting trim. "Join me in an afternoon drink?" Ackerman asked, motioning to a well-stocked bar cart. Determined to stay a shade soberer than Lester, Paul asked for a Tio Pepe. As he watched his host bend over the cart to pour out a stiff sherry in a highball glass, while suggesting a cube or two of ice to fight off the fierce July heat, Paul found it hard to remind himself that he was in the presence of a man who had just lost his wife in an inexplicable accident. Ackerman's relaxed mood had nothing in common with the brave good humor Paul had so often encountered in condolence calls when the bereaved draw on all their social resources to put the visitor at ease. Lester's nonchalance was of another order entirely. Paul would have been hard-pressed to decide whether it should be ascribed to indifference, resiliency, or a calculated effort to disarm him.

Lester handed Paul his sherry and suggested he would be comfortable on a couch of doubtful color related to the greens or blues and sadly in need of new springs. Paul's quick

glance around the room told him that if home is where the
heart is, the hearts of the Ackermans had resided elsewhere.

Lester did not take a seat but paced up and down in front
of Paul as he spoke.

"Professor Prye, let me make this visit easier for you. First
of all, don't be embarrassed talking about my wife. I don't
know whether you got to know her at all at the club, but she
wasn't the type that would have gone in for hushed tones.
Her death was a terrible thing, such a waste and so unnecessary. It is a great loss to me; we were very close in our own
way. You're going to be polite now, I see it on your face, but
we don't have to kid each other. You can't have spent much
time at the club without hearing about Melanie. Most of it's
probably not true, but she got around, she was wonderfully
attractive, don't you think?

"So far I've told you nothing you don't know, but let me
add this: I have nothing to blame her for. We both led our
own lives and that was our understanding from the beginning. So don't be embarrassed about asking me what's on
your mind. You're not going to find out much about the
stupid condolence notes by acting polite."

Lester paused after this surprising torrent of words. But
should it have been surprising? Paul thought. The news
report said Ackerman was a retired lawyer, and here he is
stalking and haranguing me as if I'm in a jury box.

Paul sensed that what Lester had said was only a prologue
to his main theme, so he waited for him to continue.

"So if we end up talking about Melanie's love affairs—or
the love affairs the Alumni think she had—that isn't going to
bother me and it shouldn't bother you either. I've got just one
subject that's off limits and that's Melanie's death. I've already
been through all that with a very irritating police detective
who I'm convinced has been sicced on me by the club. I've
already told the reporters what I have to say about her fall,
and anything else the club wants to know they can find out
when I bring my lawsuit. They're not going to head that off
by cooking up a fake homicide investigation."

"Homicide's not my game," Paul said, feeling his face

flush suddenly as he realized the unintended depth of his lie. "That is, it is a subject in which I suppose I have an uncommon interest, but it's not what brings me here today. The club has asked me to try to track down the source of the letters to which you've referred. But I hope you'll bear with me because, try as I will to toe the line, I think the letters may have something to do with Mrs. Ackerman's actions on Bessarabian Night."

"For example?" Ackerman asked warily, standing still now but satisfying his need for movement by rattling the ice in his glass.

"I guess I should ask you, to begin with, whether Mrs. Ackerman received an anonymous letter."

"She told me she did, but she didn't offer to show it to me. We respected each other's privacy, as I've already indicated, so I didn't ask to see it."

"Did she tell you anything about its contents?"

Ackerman's reply came right on the heels of Paul's question. "Yes, she did. She told me it was a condolence note expressing sympathy for the death of a man the writer strongly implied had been one of Melanie's lovers. Let me volunteer once again, Professor Prye; Melanie didn't identify the man who was named in the letter, though she said that he was very much alive."

"Are you sure of that?" Paul asked in a manner so unfocused as to leave Ackerman quite at a loss.

"Sure that she didn't identify the man? Absolutely. It wouldn't have been our style; it wasn't necessary for me to know, and we didn't cross-examine each other. I do not want to imply," Ackerman added with a smile, "that this is what you're doing now."

"No, I didn't mean that. What I wondered is whether you are certain that a man was named at all; Mrs. Ackerman told a friend that the letter purported to console her on her own coming death."

"What a bizarre idea; either your other informant got it wrong or Melanie thought it judicious to be less than frank. There is, of course, another possibility, Professor Prye, and that is that this friend of Melanie's you're quoting bears watching."

"Thanks for the warning," Paul said. "I accept the fact that Mrs. Ackerman did not mention the name of the man identified in the letter as her lover. And you've told me in your opening comments that I need not treat your wife's relationships as a sensitive subject. Can you tell me then whether Mrs. Ackerman had any attachments among the members of the Alumni Club?"

Lester responded with no more show of emotion than if he'd been asked his golf handicap, and perhaps with less emotion. "I think for a little while she had something going with John Richardson. But I wouldn't call it an attachment; from what I've heard about Richardson I think Melanie may have had a lot of competition."

"Was there anyone other than Richardson?"

"Could be, but I didn't keep score."

Paul was right. The subject did mean less to him than his golf handicap.

"Were you in the city when your wife died, Mr. Ackerman? I know you weren't at the club."

Ackerman turned his back to Paul and placed his empty glass on the bar cart, then slowly faced him again.

"Are we getting into homicide now, Professor Prye?"

"I wouldn't have thought so, but I did tell you in candor that it would be hard to draw a bright line. But hear me out, you may misunderstand me. I wasn't surprised to read that you weren't at the club because I understand you're not wild about its social life. In fact, I've heard that you do quite a bit of camping during the summer."

"Camping, shooting, that's right. In fact, the weekend before Melanie's death I'd been down in North Carolina hunting wild pig. I got back late Wednesday afternoon in time to see Melanie off for the party. I even helped her do the clasps on her gypsy outfit."

On another occasion Paul might have been struck by the blandness with which Ackerman described his last moments with his wife, but now he was totally absorbed in his own line of questioning. "And did Melanie ask you for anything before she left?"

Ackerman looked puzzled, as well he might. "Can you give me a hint what you're driving at?"

"I wondered whether she might have asked to borrow some of your camping equipment," Paul suggested awkwardly.

Ackerman eyed his guest with new interest. "As a matter of fact, she did. She told me that the club was having its usual summer miseries with power failures and asked to borrow my flashlight."

"What kind of flashlight was it?"

"It's a heavy-duty flashlight. Quite a load for Melanie to carry, but as usual she was wearing her shoulder bag, so she put the flashlight into the bag. I guess it wasn't as bad as carrying a backpack or toting kids around the way these young girls do nowadays."

Ackerman scratched his head reflectively. Was this another trial lawyer's gesture? Paul wondered, only to be surprised when Ackerman brought the conversation to an end on a rare personal note: "Of course, Mr. Prye, Melanie and I never had any children."

Alice peered at Paul satirically through the tall bread sticks that screened her from a better view. They sat opposite each other at a small table in a restaurant across from Lincoln Center.

"Let's see whether I'm getting this straight; it's your theory that the weapon with which Melanie was struck was Lester Ackerman's camping flashlight. I am also to believe that you sprung this brilliant discovery on Dave Emmerich this afternoon and he has not yet sent around the little men in the white suits."

Paul nodded as he shot a covered glance at his watch. They still had almost an hour until curtain time for *Candide* at the State Theatre.

"That's right. I think Dave is pretty enthusiastic about the idea."

Alice decided to try one of the bread sticks. She didn't have to worry about the calories and she would certainly be able to see Paul better. "And what is it precisely that excites him so?"

Paul overlooked the sarcasm. "It all fits, really. Lester saw her put the flashlight in her bag when she left for the club. It wasn't there when the police examined the bag and it hasn't been found anywhere else on the club premises."

"They haven't been looking all that long."

"You may be wrong about that. I get the impression that Dave has been hunting pretty intensively for a weapon ever since he had his first conversation with the pathologist who did the postmortem. That's how he came across Dan Twitchell."

"Dan who?" asked Alice, gnawing on her bread stick.

Paul summarized what Dave had told him when he returned Paul's telephone call to Police Plaza. In the course of their inspection of the club building, Dave and a pair of his detectives had this morning visited the ninth floor. It was a backwater of the club Paul had never seen (until his own visit after Dave's call). Most of the floor was taken up by an enormous dormitory made available at modest charge to undergraduates who were visiting New York and might not be able to afford the ever-escalating hotel rates. It seemed to Paul, when he surveyed the large joyless room with row upon row of bunk beds, that the authority of Victor Baines and his House Committee did not reach the ninth floor. The place looked like a nineteenth-century doss house, as pictured in Gustave Doré's nightmarish etchings of London.

It was in the dormitory that Dave Emmerich came upon Dan Twitchell, a wiry young man in a sweatshirt and shorts. The three detectives must not have been as unobtrusive as they thought; the student promptly introduced himself and launched into his story about Bessarabian Night.

"Dave listened to Twitchell with particular interest, because what he had to say seemed to suggest an explanation for a troublesome problem."

"And what is it that has troubled our friend Emmerich?"

"The same thing that's puzzled you and me: whether the murderer left the club before the police arrived."

Alice scoffed. "You know my views already. Why hang around when it would have been perfectly easy to slip away in the darkness and confusion?"

"Well, according to Emmerich, it hadn't seemed as easy as that. They placed the time of Melanie's fall at one-ten A.M. The police arrived about twenty minutes later. During all that time, the doorman sat at his station near the front door and saw nobody leave."

"How could he see anything in the dark?"

"The management is more efficient that you might suppose. The doorman had been furnished with a candlestick and lighted it as soon as the power went out."

"I'm still unimpressed," Alice said. "If the doorman's the same drowsy type who greeted us when we arrived and hasn't found a cab since the invention of the horseless carriage, I wouldn't bet a lot on his attention span."

"Well, put it down to naïveté, if you will, but Dave seemed to think the doorman's story was pretty reliable. That's why he was glad to run into this unexpected witness in the ninth-floor dormitory. It seems that young Twitchell is a confirmed midnight jogger. Around one-fifteen Thursday morning he was returning to the club from a run in Central Park."

"Really! The boy's parents should be notified at once."

"Not everyone is as protective as Mother Prye. In any event he was just about to enter the club when he practically ran into a man who seemed to be leaving in a hurry."

"At the front door?" asked Alice. "Then how does that square with the evidence of your sharp-eyed doorman?"

"Shame on you, Alice; you've forgotten the rules. Joggers don't have front-door privileges; they use the jogger's door near the reception desk."

"You mean to tell me that, while I thought—at least until

Bessarabian Night—I was living here in semi-security, un-regulated athletes have been popping in and out of the lobby in the small hours of the morning?"

"It's not as bad as that. The night receptionist is supposed to keep her eye on the door, but she seemed to be away from the desk at the moment in question. Anyway, Twitchell told Dave he practically collided with a man leaving the jogger's door."

"Fantastic, and how was the guy dressed? I hope it wasn't a Vlad the Impaler, we had far too many of them, but I suppose it couldn't have been a Vlad, or Twitchell would have been run through with one of those ugly-looking stakes."

"Unfortunately, Dave couldn't get much help on that point. Twitchell believes that the man was in shirt sleeves and could have been carrying a coat rolled up under an arm, but he is not sure of that. By the way, according to what Dave has learned, this description would fit almost any of the men at the party by one in the morning. It had gotten unbearably hot by then, and just about all the men, costumed or not, had peeled down to their shirts. But Twitchell had a better reason than that for guessing the man was a runner, and that's what tied his story in with what Ackerman told me. Twitchell told Dave that the man he bumped into was carrying an enormous flashlight which blinded him when it shone in his face. He almost felt that the fellow had done it on purpose."

By agreement the Pryes dropped the subject of the Ack-erman case until *Candide* was over and they had returned to their room. Then Alice said, "The truce is over. I make the drinks and you tell me where we go detecting tomorrow. You've simply got to come up with a solution before Dave, I insist on it, and I don't just mean the letters; you have to catch the murderer as well. So far you are way ahead of Dave. It's you that came up with the flashlight, and the best he could produce was this Twit—what is the twit's name again?"

"Twitchell," Paul called from the bathroom where he'd

gone in search of their liquor supply. He brought her the vodka bottle, which was almost empty. "We're running low; you don't suppose the maid's been at the bottle?"

"It must be something like that," Alice said, glad to go along with the polite explanation.

"You were asking about tomorrow. I think it's about time for a showdown with our friend Rodney Baker. I hope you don't mind the same old surroundings, but I've made a brunch reservation at the SoHo joint."

"That's fine; I think there is a sidewalk sale in the neighborhood."

"The rest of Sunday is at leisure, but I wonder whether you can break away from the word processor for a couple of days; on Monday I was thinking of transporting you across state lines."

"Whatever for? I thought they used to have a law about that."

"That, too, of course, but I also had in mind calling on a key witness."

"Is it a mysterious woman?" Alice asked hopefully.

"No, I'm sorry about that, but it is a category of informants who are often quite as fruitful; we are going to see a disgruntled ex-employee."

The brunch got off to a good start. Rodney Baker had some good news for them.

"I spoke to John Richardson again yesterday. He tells me that he will be glad to see you later this week. I would suggest you give him a call on Thursday to set something up."

"That's great, Rodney," Paul said. "What do you think finally did the trick?"

Rodney went through some silent neck-stretching exercises before he replied. "I always thought he would come around if Vic Baines and I kept after him. It's Baines who convinced him, I think. Richardson's always been close to the House Committee."

"I suppose that Melanie's death couldn't have had anything to do with it," Alice suggested. She was beginning to find Baker's discretion unbearable.

Paul glared at her and felt compelled to redouble his own show of gratitude. "Nonsense, Alice, I'm sure that Rodney can read Richardson like a book after all these years, and that persistence has finally paid off. I'll follow up as you suggest, Rodney, on Thursday. Alice and I are planning a little trip tomorrow, but we'll be back before then."

A question began to form on Rodney's lips but he suffocated it with a mouthful of French toast. After a while he said, "Well, I believe that scheduling the Richardson interview was the last item on my current punch list. Is there anything else I can do for you?"

"As a matter of fact, there are two matters that require urgent attention." Trying to avoid meeting Rodney's worried look, Paul prefaced his request with an explanation.

"I don't want to overstate the importance of my mission and I will repeat this morning what I've said many times, namely that you can call me off the trail of the Friend any time you want to. But you haven't done that, and I can suggest one very good reason why you would not want to do so: the stakes of the game have risen. You started me out to track down anonymous letters that looked to you and others at the club like death threats, and now a mysterious death has followed."

Rodney waited for Paul to continue. "I say 'mysterious death' because nobody's officially called it murder and the story's disappeared from the media. But it's an open secret at the club that the police are far from satisfied and that Lieutenant Emmerich is continuing to investigate the matter. I say that the time has come for the club management to help him and my own inquiry in an effective manner."

Rodney looked vigilant. "And how would we be able to help other than by showing willingness to answer questions, as I believe we have all done?"

"That's helpful, of course, but not what I have in mind."

"What would you suggest?"

"I am suggesting, and indeed have already proposed to Lieutenant Emmerich, that printing samples be obtained from everyone who was at the club on Bessarabian Night."

"Do you know what you are saying?" Rodney's voice rose with unusual emotion. "There must have been five hundred people at the party."

Paul lowered his voice to emphasize Rodney's discomfort. "Not quite five hundred actually, four hundred fifty-nine, if the seating chart that Brian Kennedy was good enough to give me was complete."

Baker's narrow range of facial expression was tested severely. A trace of panic crept into his voice.

"You can't be serious. Are you suggesting that we subject four hundred sixty members and guests to a test that can mean only that we regard them capable of poison-pen letters and possibly homicide as well? It's going to be hard to sell the notion that we may be harboring a murderer."

Paul was not inclined to show mercy. "And yet you don't find that impossible to believe, do you, Rodney? When you called me in to start my inquiry, you must have thought at least that the person who was sending out these addled condolence notes was capable of murder. Let me go one step further. I don't think you're the only person at the club who had that worry, or you would never have taken it upon yourself to call me in. Am I wrong?"

Rodney made no objection.

"And I'll tell you what else I think: that you and your fellow worriers, whoever they may be, have never told me everything that's on your minds, all that leads you to think now that the august Alumni Club of New York City may be, as you put it, harboring a murderer. So I've another request to make of you, a request you would have had from me a lot earlier if I had the guts you need to be a detective in the real world and not just in a library."

Visibly Rodney braced himself against the new demand

that would be made of him. Paul concluded: "Rodney, I'd like to meet with the Oversight Committee."

Baker was not quite ready for Paul's request when it finally came.

"I can make no promises; that goes without saying. But I'll make your wishes known."

CHAPTER 9

Alice's patience with Paul's secrecy was beginning to wear thin; they were turning off the highway at the exit to La Guardia and he still had not announced their destination. "This is not exactly my idea of a mystery tour, if that's what you have in mind; to please me you'd have to start me off with a lei and macadamia nuts. Or perhaps I wrong you, we're not off to the islands, I presume?"

"No," said Paul, uncowed by her show of ferocity, "you'll have to settle for Sarasota."

"And whom are we to see there, the man who's got Melanie's flashlight, who ran out the jogger's door with it and never stopped running until he reached Florida?"

Paul finally told her, fearing his revelation would be an anticlimax. "As a matter of fact, we're going to visit Ross Lytton."

"Who the hell is that? The name sounds like a conglomerate or a men's shirt."

Paul was beginning to bank on an arduous trip. "Don't you remember? He's the associate manager of the club who's retiring, or I think being forced into retirement."

"Isn't that against the law?"

Paul looked ahead with frustration as their radio cab joined a long line of cars that were inching forward towards their departure terminal. "Apparently the law doesn't apply to the Alumni Club, but what if it does, that's just the point. The man may be mad enough about it to tell us something interesting."

"What makes you think so?" Alice's curiosity was beginning to overpower her early-morning crossness.

"An odd source, really. I got a call on Saturday from Miles Corbett's friend Aileen Scroop. I don't think that she was calling from the apartment, but if she was, Corbett probably wasn't around. She certainly talked without constraint."

"And what did this model of candor tell you?"

The cab was still crawling along in thickening traffic when Paul answered. "She started with polite questions about the progress of my inquiry. When I told her that the light was not yet shining at the end of the tunnel, she suggested I talk to Lytton and gave me his address."

"But why's Lytton our man?"

"Ms. Scroop strongly implied that his retirement was not of his choosing and that he might be in a mood to talk."

The Pryes boarded their plane a half hour late and sat on the runway for another hour. Alice uttered a few heartfelt curses against deregulation and returned to the subject of Ross Lytton.

"Why do you call him a 'witness'? It seems to me that if he feels his retirement is an injustice, he might be as good a suspect as you've uncovered. He'd have a perfect motive to attack the club bigwigs in the condolence notes, to disrupt the peace of the clubhouse with all those irritating practical jokes, and then to eliminate Melanie when he gave himself away in his note to her and she confronted him on the gallery. By the way, was Lytton at the club on Bessarabian Night?"

"I think so," Paul said. "At least, his name was on the seating chart; of course, he didn't sit up above with the Alumni gods. But, Alice, you disappoint me, I thought you were absolutely persuaded that the Friend is a woman; at last account, I believe, you'd figured it was Melanie."

Alice had a sudden inspiration that enabled her to defend her old bastion. "In a way, I was right, you see. Maybe the Friend wasn't *actually* a woman, I may grant you that for purposes of argument, but couldn't it be that our disgruntled old-line staffer wanted people to think so? All the other tricks—the adulterated wine, the erased squash dates—were plainly unisex, but there was no better way than poison-pen letters to pin the whole subversive campaign on a woman. So old Lytton found a perfect cover for his misdeeds, the very one clubmen all over the world will give a standing ovation—blame it on a female! And it might have worked if he hadn't written that fatal note to Melanie, which didn't fool her for a moment." Alice paused for a radiant smile of self-congratulation. "Well, what do you think of my solution?"

"You're satirizing your unsuccessful husband, that's what I think, but there's something in what you've said all the same."

During their flight Alice pursued her initiative. "Okay, so Lytton's another possibility, but you've got a flock of perfectly good suspects already. Isn't it time to summarize?"

She feared that Paul, left to his own devices, might continue gathering data forever. When asked for his selection among the most fashionable candidates for Jack the Ripper, he would always respond that we did not know enough and likely never would; that Jack was probably None of the Above.

With resignation Paul suggested that she proceed, and she gladly accepted.

"First, there are the outsiders with possible grudges against the club and its members. You've already ruled out the rejected applicant Ben Tolliver; I'm glad of that. The fake Charlie Benson, then? We don't even know where he is. Then how about Ackerman, the jealous husband who hated Melanie and her reputed lovers? Melanie would have recognized his writing."

Paul shook his head. "You're stereotyping him. I don't think Ackerman was jealous. And I can't see the doting

Vance Parry as a 'reputed lover' of Melanie's. Yet Marian Morrison received a letter."

"How about Lytton, who has a grudge against club management and may not have approved of Melanie's behavior?"

"I reserve judgment on Lytton. That's why we're on the way to Sarasota."

"Okay." Alice took up a second category. "Then there's the targets of the poison-pen letters. Great suspects there, I think."

Paul smiled. "As the Friend or the murderer?"

Alice, enjoying her mental exercise, refused clarification. "As either or both perhaps. How about Miles Corbett, for starters? A malicious writer since college days, he's just the type to dash off these condolence letters without a qualm, and frankly I can also see him running after Melanie."

"You're just showing your prejudice against aging campus radicals," said Paul, taunting her. She was much more liberal than he was.

"Aileen Scroop doesn't trust him. Why else did she give you the Lytton hint on the sly? But I'll move on. I have trouble with Parry, as you do; he sacrificed so much to his love affair with Marian Morrison that I don't visualize him in a clubhouse romance. But what about John Richardson? The Friend wasn't subtle about his reputation with women, and even your 'non-jealous' Lester Ackerman suspected he was one of Melanie's flames."

"I pass on Richardson until I've had a chance to talk to him."

Alice seized on the point. "And isn't that another strike against him? Why is he the only victim of the Friend who's held out against seeing you? Isn't it sort of like taking the Fifth Amendment?"

Paul did not reply to her question, but instead asked, "Does that exhaust our suspects?"

"You know perfectly well it doesn't; I'm well aware you are not overlooking the club bureaucrats who, with varying degrees of enthusiasm, are supposedly aiding your investigation."

"And how do you rate the suspects in this group?" Paul asked.

Alice ticked them off on her fingers as she spoke. "I hope it's not our friend Rodney Baker, the 'trustee type.' I don't say this because we know him socially, but he's the guy who invited you to investigate. That makes him the 'least likely person,' and I hate it when the murderer turns out to be least likely, don't you."

Covering the inadequacy of her analysis, Alice moved on to Vic Baines. "More promising, perhaps. Baines is the eternal house chairman, obviously attached to the club, very likely to be offended by Melanie's affairs and the public disgraces of Richardson and Parry.

"Then there's Ralph Murray, the Admissions Committee chief. He's probably a rising star at the club and may well have it in for the older generation of leaders. You've told me he can't stand Baines. Nobody's paired him with Melanie, but he looks like a vain man, and I wouldn't rule out a little extracurricular activity—in addition to the mandatory squash."

"I see you've left your new admirer, Brian Kennedy, for last."

"You're right, so I have. He's obviously got a certain appeal, all that cocktail-party charm and a streak of rebelliousness that's refreshing—at least to me. But maybe the Alumni Club doesn't go much for rebels and that's why Brian doesn't get the big posts."

"He's chairman of the Athletics Committee," Paul reminded her.

"That's true," Alice replied quickly, "and I seem to recall that it was to the domain of his committee on the eighth floor that you were invited for the fake squash date.

"Well, there you have it, all wrapped up for you. Are you ready to choose, or will you answer 'None of the Above'?"

Paul remained silent.

★ ★ ★

When they were shown into their suite on Longboat Key with a balcony overlooking the golf course, Alice propounded a new riddle to Paul: "How do they keep them staying at the Alumni Club after they've see Sarasota?"

"It's a major mystery," Paul agreed, "but I suggest we worry about it tomorrow. We've got to get some sleep, because Lytton insists on our calling at the ungodly hour of nine A.M."

"He's probably got a full day planned," Alice surmised, "he must have fallen behind in his correspondence."

The next morning the Pryes killed their box of Wheat Thins and headed out towards the address Lytton had given. "Quite a retirement neighborhood our associate manager has picked out for himself," Alice said as they drove past the sports clubs and condominia that lined Gulf of Mexico Drive. "How do you explain it, Paul, fine old family or fingers in the till?"

The question resolved itself as they approached the north tip of the key and turned east into a side road not far from a stone-crab restaurant that the Pryes remembered from previous visits. Slowing down, they passed a row of modest frame houses that had been built long before the developers seized upon the southern end of Longboat. Lytton's house, a cottage really, was even less imposing than most of its neighbors but was well situated in a palm grove where the road dead-ended.

A note, on half-letter paper of the Alumni Club, was Scotch-taped to the front door:

"Please knock and walk right in. I'm expecting you."

Paul did as instructed. They found themselves in a central room that occupied most of the house, except for a kitchenette adjoining on the left and a bedroom and bath that were probably beyond two closed doors on the right. Lytton sat facing them behind a desk that had been placed in front of a window which overlooked a small back garden.

Lytton did not rise to meet them but summoned a formal

smile that faded quickly. "Mr. and Mrs. Prye, of course. Make yourselves comfortable, at least as comfortable as you can. I don't often have guests. I assume you've had breakfast?" It was a rhetorical question.

Lytton had not found time in his career to learn the art of small talk; he waited for Paul to begin.

"It was nice of you to let us visit."

Lytton parried mechanically. "I'd say it is flattering for you to come all this way to see an old retiree. But I must warn you, I'm afraid you're going to be disappointed."

Paul took him on. "Why is that?"

"I must confess a secret vice. Have you ever in your travels come upon a nun who's reading Agatha Christie instead of her missal? If so, you'll not be surprised to learn that even an associate manager of the Alumni Club—or rather former associate manager, I'll have to get used to that—reads mystery novels from time to time. The detective arrives to interview an employee who's just been put out to pasture. The old fool's just overflowing with grievances against management and just the man to come up with startling revelations. But let me assure you it doesn't always work that way in real life, Mr. Prye, at least not with me. It isn't that easy to unlearn many long years of discretion just because the last paycheck is about to arrive."

Paul guessed that Alice was laughing silently at him; though they were both academics she didn't share his foible of underestimating people.

"I don't want you to breach any confidences, Mr. Lytton," Paul answered, "but I *was* hoping that you could speak with more detachment than some of the club members we've talked to about these condolence notes. After all, you haven't received one."

Lytton remained silent, so Paul went on. "What do you think's on the mind of the letter writer, a person who, as you know, signs himself as the 'Friend from the Alumni Club'?"

"I can't believe you had to come all the way to Florida to find that out. The writer's someone who doesn't like the movers and shakers at the club."

Paul nodded. "But who is it that moves and shakes the club? That's what I thought you could tell us as realistically as anyone. Isn't it the Oversight Committee?"

It seemed to the Pryes that Lytton felt comfortable with the question. The conversation did not seem to be taking a turn he had feared, calling on him to disclose administrative secrets or records that had been committed to his safekeeping. "I believe you are correct, but understand that it is only my impression. I have only worked with the formal committees."

Paul acknowledged the disclaimer. "Can you tell us who's on the Oversight Committee?"

"Even that would be a guess. I've never been told, but I'd have to be blind not to form some pretty good guesses. The chairmen of the major committees are ordinarily members, not necessarily ex officio, but certainly those who've held committee chairs for years. Then, too, officers or past officers who are particularly influential."

"Let me try to apply that learning. How about Richardson, Corbett, and Parry?"

"Richardson clearly, he's the most powerful man at the club, and Corbett almost surely. His father was president of the University, and even though Miles Corbett is something of a black sheep, these strong college ties count for a lot at the club. I'm not certain about Mr. Parry, though. I don't think he likes committee work, though he is very generous in his financial support. I've not often seen him around on days when I've thought the Oversight Committee was gathering."

"And where do they meet?"

"The place varies, but they don't usually meet in the club itself, although they often favor one of the conference rooms in the bank next door."

Paul returned to the membership of the Oversight Committee, which he was jotting down in his notebook.

"Would the current president of the club be a member?"

"Mr. Preswick? Most likely not, he's had a number of

official posts over the years, but he's turned out to be pretty much an absentee president."

"Which of the committees would be regarded as major committees?"

"Admissions would certainly be the most significant, followed closely by House, and Athletics and Games."

"Their current chairmen are Murray, Baines, and Kennedy. Would they all be on the Oversight Committee?"

"Probably the first two," Lytton said, "but I'd have to wonder about Mr. Kennedy. He's regarded as a nay-sayer, and that doesn't make him popular with the old-timers."

"He seems to be a moving spirit among the Bessarabians," Paul said, hoping that his change of direction was not as obvious as he feared.

"Yes, and he's been particularly kind about inviting me to their annual event, even this year, when there is no longer any practical reason to show me extraordinary courtesy."

"I did not know you were there," Paul lied and left it to Lytton to pick up the thread.

"I'm going to disappoint you again, Mr. Prye," Lytton said, reviving his unwarming smile. "I left before Mrs. Ackerman's unfortunate accident."

"What can you tell us about Mrs. Ackerman?" Paul asked, anxious to emphasize that he was treating their host as an information source.

"A very popular member," Lytton responded, echoing the appraisal Ralph Murray had recently made. "It's not my business to deal in club gossip, if that was your expectation, but I can say that her vivacity was easy to misread. Indeed, I believe that some of our members may have misread it, but Mrs. Ackerman was very deft; she would have known how to set them straight without making a scene."

Mr. Lytton left no doubt that he regarded avoiding "scenes" at the club as the highest good, and that he had said all he could be persuaded to tell about Melanie Ackerman.

When the conversation ended and the Pryes prepared to go, Ross Lytton let his arms fall and groped along the floor behind his chair. He drew up a pair of crutches and painfully rose to accompany his guests to the door. On the way he explained apologetically:

"It's my arthritis, you see. It keeps kicking up these days more than it used to. But it didn't interfere with the performance of my duties at the club, I can assure you of that. Still, I know the Oversight Committee in its wisdom saw it differently, and who am I to quarrel with the Oversight Committee?"

Lytton showed a flicker of amusement as he caught the Pryes exchanging surprised looks. He had a final barb for them.

"Brian Kennedy, though, remained a perfect gentleman. He knows I've had a little trouble getting around lately, so when he invited me to Bessarabian Night this year, he was good enough not to seat me in the gallery."

At four o'clock next morning Alice asked Paul whether he was awake. When he didn't answer she stabbed a well-targeted index finger into the small of his back; it never failed.

"Mmm," he protested.

"I've been thinking about the Friend and Melanie's note. I've had to, now that your 'disgruntled ex-employee' is out of the picture."

Paul rubbed his eyes and groaned, but she knew he was listening.

"The way I see it now is that my Monday-morning thinking was deduction at its best. The Friend is a man who wrote these notes hoping he'd be taken for a woman. Finally, he made the big mistake of writing to Melanie, who was smarter than the others and saw through his anonymity in a minute. How? I'm not sure and maybe we'll never know unless the Friend helps us somehow by another big mistake, so I'm not going to worry about that puzzle for the time being. What's deprived me of my rest is quite another question, namely the one that's teased us both: Whose death was lamented in Melanie's note and why was she so secretive about that detail? She even went out of her way to indulge in mystification on that score, telling her husband and Aileen

Scroop the note consoled her on the death of a third person and informing Kennedy on Bessarabian Night that the Friend predicted her own death. This morning my dreaming thoughts tell me which version was right, and why."

Now Paul was clearly awake. "And the verdict is?"

"The first version was correct. As in the other notes, the Friend consoled her on the death of a man, and it was a man he asserted was her current lover, Tom Simmons."

"Well, why then wouldn't Melanie be proud to show the note around to all and sundry? Both times we saw her and Simmons together she seemed to be trying to stake her claim of ownership in the sight of the entire club."

Alice was beginning to think her cleverness was wasted on him, at least before breakfast. "You'll never make much of a detective unless you become a better observer of the mating game. Hasn't it been obvious to you that Melanie was making no progress at all with Simmons? If she'd shown the note to anyone, she'd have been totally humiliated. Come to think of it, that's probably what the Friend intended; he's probably got sharper eyes than you. Well, it's rebuttal time. Do you give up?"

Paul's surrender was partial. "I can follow you much of the way, but I come out differently. I think that she told Kennedy the truth; the note prophesied her own death and that's why she hunted the Friend down on Bessarabian Night with fire in her eyes, and unfortunately with an oversized flashlight in her hand which he chivalrously took from her to lead the way."

"But why would he have written her a note so much crueler than those he sent to the other women?"

Paul answered with assurance, probably with more than he felt. "Because at worst he disliked the others—or perhaps I should say the husband or lover of the others. But I think he must have hated Melanie."

CHAPTER 10

The second of the Alumni Club murders was committed on Tuesday, while the Pryes were in Florida.

According to their statements to Dave Emmerich, Miles Corbett and Bart Tucker, the chairman of the club's Wine and Food Committee, were the first to discover the body. They had arrived early for a club meeting that was to be held at 3:30 P.M. at Conference Room B of the Midtown National Bank, which adjoined the club premises. They were surprised to find the door to the conference room locked (it was usually left open well in advance of the meeting hour), and went to obtain a key in the administrative offices of the bank. Returning to Conference Room B, they opened the door and stumbled across a corpse that lay prone on the floor. They kept their composure and did not turn the body over. Besides, it was not necessary; they could tell at a glance that it was Rodney Baker.

Emmerich filled the Pryes in on the details when he faced them across the meeting table of Conference Room B on Wednesday afternoon.

"It was a meeting of the Oversight Committee, of course, that was scheduled," Emmerich told them. "Strange to hear the words come out so loud and clear after the way these fellows have been horsing me around."

"You're sure they really said 'Oversight Committee'?" Alice couldn't believe it. "You didn't hear them say 'our thing' or something like that?"

"No, they're past that by now."

Paul had taken out his notebook. "And after Corbett and Tucker found Rodney's body, did the other troops arrive?"

"In force. Corbett and Tucker were only a few minutes early." He read a list of the committee members to the Pryes. There were only a few surprises. They would not have thought that the Wine and Food Committee would have merited representation. Lytton had been wrong about Preswick; he was on the Oversight Committee and had flown in from Martha's Vineyard for the meeting. On the other hand, Lytton had guessed correctly that Parry, despite his financial clout, and Kennedy, because of his nonconformity, were not on the Oversight roster. Other names meant nothing to the Pryes; in general the remaining members were past officers and substantial donors.

Kennedy turned to an even more intriguing subject, the means of death. Baker had been struck by a heavy object whose nature or characteristics could not be determined. It was certain only that the murderer had taken the weapon away, for nothing that could have served his purpose was found in the room and the bank staff confirmed that none of the room's furnishings was missing.

The injuries that caused Baker's death did not help the police identify the weapon that had been used. A blow, or more likely a series of blows, had caused a fracture of the left temporal bone and a rupture of the middle meningeal artery, with attendant hematoma and epidural bleeding.

"In other words," Paul summarized, "most of the bleeding was internal."

"That's right," Emmerich said, jarred loose of his postmortem lingo. "There was only a little external blood and a dark crease in the area of the temple that marks the principal point of impact."

"Does the crease tell us anything about the shape of the weapon?"

Emmerich shook his head. "Not much, I'm afraid. But there is something else, fortunately."

The Pryes had been looking forward to this revelation. The morning's *Times* had reported that the police had found near the murder scene evidence (the nature of which they were not prepared to disclose) that they hoped would enable them to trace the weapon.

"What do you make of this?" Emmerich slid a colored photograph across the table. "We found this in a wastebasket in the corridor."

The Pryes studied the picture. It showed a brown fabric bag closed by drawstrings with small golden baubles. Paul shrugged but Alice said,

"It's a non-tarnish silver bag. We've got lots of them at home. We call ours 'Pacific' cloth, because they have the manufacturer's logo on them."

Emmerich was pleased. "There was no logo here, but we reached the same conclusion. There was something on this bag, by the way, that was far more interesting."

"What's that?" Paul said, furious at Emmerich for quizzing him about a household object he'd be unlikely to identify.

"Traces of blood. I've been told today it's Baker's group. Any theories?"

"I'll bet you're thinking the same thing as I."

Emmerich smiled. "Let's hear it."

"John Donald Merrett."

"True to form, Prye, you're always predictable. Explain to Alice."

John Donald Merrett (alias Ronald Chesney) was a New Zealander who made a lethal assault on his mother-in-law, Lady Menzies, with a pewter pitcher. Paul had seen the weapon in a recent visit to Scotland Yard's Black Museum and was amazed how small it was.

"Surely silver in this instance, given the non-tarnish bag," Alice urged.

"Is it possible? What do you think?" Emmerich asked.

"The wounds seem curious," Paul replied. "I would have expected that if it were a silver pitcher or some similar object with a spout or handles, there'd be more external bruising and blood. Have you ever seen those ghastly police photos of Lady Menzies?"

"Yes, I have, but the postmortem boys tell me that the injuries they found could be consistent with blows delivered with the rounded walls of a metal vessel."

Alice began to wonder whether, like her famous namesake, she had been invited to a mad tea party. "Are you grown men telling me that a murderer waylaid Rodney Baker in the conference room and prepared himself for his murderous mission by bringing along a pitcher?"

Paul thought that in her skeptical fashion she had gone right to the heart of the matter.

"You may be closer to the truth than you know because you've made a number of unnecessary assumptions that may not be correct. First, that the murderer came to the conference room with the intention of killing Baker. Second— though I don't place as much stress on this point—that it was the murderer who brought the weapon. He may have, but we can't be sure.

"I'd like to stand back for a minute and make a broader assumption, one that we all share, I believe, but haven't put out on the table: that the man who murdered Rodney Baker is the same person who struck Melanie Ackerman with the flashlight and threw her from the club gallery. Aren't you impressed by the suggestive parallels between the two killings? The most remarkable is of course that in both cases unusual weapons were used, everyday objects that were easy to carry away from the scene of the crime without arousing curiosity.

"Now why does the murderer use these strange vanishing weapons? Is it that he's a master criminal who knows how easy it is to be done in by ballistics tests or toxicology?

"I doubt it. Isn't it more likely that neither of these murders was planned, that the killer (let's call him by his own adopted name, the Friend from the Alumni Club) has an uncontrollable temper, and that when he finds himself in a desperate situation he uses the first weapon that comes to hand? The improvisatory nature of these crimes is nowhere more apparent than in his assault on Melanie, where it was the victim herself who furnished the proverbial blunt instrument."

Alice liked the neatness of it all but she had her reservations. "So that means that it was Rodney Baker who brought in the silver pitcher or whatever it is supposed to have been?"

Paul fielded the question as if he hadn't noticed the irony. "Possibly. I don't think we should exclude that alternative, but even if the lethal object belonged to the killer, I still don't think that would indicate he planned to attack Rodney."

Paul asked Emmerich for an orientation tour of the bank premises. He believed, to the extent he could rely on his feeble sense of spatial relations, that Conference Room B (which was the starting point of their walk) was the same room in which the club meeting had been held on the previous Saturday while he was inspecting the files of the Admissions and House committees. As they left the conference room, Emmerich led them farther down the corridor to the right. Paul observed two other conference rooms across the passage and on the right side a door that led into the bank's administrative offices. A few paces farther took them to a short flight of stairs that led up to the bank lobby located on a mezzanine level. Paul noticed that the principal entrance of the bank building was a short walk from the foot of the stairway along a transverse corridor lined with cigarette counters and newsstands.

Emmerich followed the direction of Paul's gaze. "Yes, it's possible the man entered and left by that door and may not have been seen in the club at all. Is there anything more you want to see?"

"Not for the moment," Paul said, and they turned to retrace their steps up the long corridor that led back to the Alumni Club. As they reached the far end of the hallway, Paul came to a stop. He was facing the outer grille of the safe depository that was just closing for the day. Stepping closer to the grille, Paul could see a middle-aged woman sitting at the reception desk, making her final entries in the customer-access journal. Beyond her the door of the vault stood ajar, restrained by the toe of a guard slumped on a stool inside the entrance; he waited sleepily for the last two depositors to leave.

Paul stood silently for a few moments and when he could tear himself away from the grille he saw that Dave and Alice had already begun to walk on towards the connecting door that led into the club lobby. He caught up with them and suggested that they confer for a few minutes. Dave agreed, and Paul led the way to a secluded corner of the Great Hall.

Paul didn't lose a minute telling Emmerich what was on his mind. "What are you going to do about the safe depository?"

"Should I be doing anything?"

"Surely it's occurred to you that this may be where the weapon's been hidden."

"Or that it's where it was taken from," Alice added, liking Paul's idea but thinking it needed elaboration.

Emmerich gave them both a smile that exuded benevolence to amateurs. "You aren't forgetting the bank layout, I hope. It would have been perfectly possible for our man to enter and leave through the street door and just take the weapon away with him."

Paul was ready for the objection. "I don't think he could have done that under all circumstances, at least not under the conditions I propose. Isn't it possible that he was planning to attend the meeting in Conference Room B?"

Alice caught him up sharply. "You mean he was a member of the Oversight Committee?"

"That's not for us to say yet. We have no idea how they run their meetings; maybe they invite guests to give reports or to consult on matters that are before them, who knows? But what I'm suggesting is that the murderer and Baker were both to attend the three-thirty meeting and agreed to meet earlier for some advance discussion. If I'm right that the killer struck Baker down in a sudden rage, he couldn't have simply walked off with his weapon into the teeming metropolis, as you suggest, Dave, because he would have been missed at the meeting. So he looks around for the nearest place to dispose of the weapon and the first thing that popped into his mind was the safe depository."

Paul's thoughts sped on. "Or the idea may have come to him even more naturally than that. Suppose he brought the object with him in the silver bag, intending to deposit it before the meeting began. Murder was not quite what he had in mind, but it took little adjustment in his thinking for him to slip down the hall, as he had always planned to do, and to deposit the pitcher, whatever it was, in his box."

"There was at least one change he seems to have made in his arrangements," Alice noted, breaking into his monologue. "If there'd been no murder and he'd gone to deposit his silver, wouldn't he have left it in the non-tarnish bag?"

Paul reflected for a moment. "You have a point there, there must have been some reason why he felt insecure about the bag. Dave, you tell us there were bloodstains on the bag. They were a lot brighter then, and maybe he was afraid they'd be noticed when he signed the register. Or maybe that wasn't it, and it was just that he didn't much like the thought of stowing away in his personal deposit box a bloody bag that might be discovered there and incriminate him as surely as if it bore his autograph."

Emmerich was having trouble with the theory, so Alice gave it a psychological twist. "Dave, you'd have to live with Paul to know, as I do, where he gets this kind of notion. He's the guiltiest man I've ever known, he probably cheated in a game of hide and seek at his first birthday party. He's always dreaming that he's committed some secret crime years ago and that the police find the telltale evidence in his night-table drawer. So please accept a wife's plea. Humor him about the depository or, like Macbeth, he shall sleep no more."

Emmerich turned to Paul. "What would you have us do?"

Paul was not fooled. He suspected that Emmerich had the safe depository on his mind when he led the Pryes there during the tour of the bank. It was another of the detective's annoying little tests, like showing the picture of the silver bag. Emmerich knew, as he did, that it was far from unknown for professional killers to hide murder guns in safe-deposit boxes. They'd read the same cases, and there's nothing new under the red sun of crime.

"Of course you'd quiz the receptionist and the guards but I'd go beyond that. The access record for the day of the crime should be reviewed."

"For names of the Oversight Committee members?" Alice asked.

"I'd cast a broader net than that. I'd check the journal against the club roster."

"That's doable," Emmerich said, making his response sound hypothetical.

Paul went on. "The next part gets a little beyond my depth. If I found that any Alumni went into their boxes that afternoon, I'd find a way to open those boxes. The point is, though, Dave: Can you do that without giving notice to the box holders and blowing the whole investigation in advance? I seem to remember from some of the safe-deposit cases we've talked about that the police need a court order."

Emmerich flashed another of his tolerant smiles. "That may be right technically, but I don't think it would be necessary in this case. You see, I've looked into the matter this morning, just on an exploratory basis, you understand, and I find that a number of the bank officers are Alumni. I wouldn't be surprised if they'd let us take a look-see on an informal basis."

Paul couldn't have been more pleased, he'd been right in thinking that Emmerich was just the man for the Alumni Club case. Smart, discreet, and not too scrupulous.

John Richardson called Paul late Wednesday afternoon. "I promised Rod Baker I would see you this week. When he was killed, my first thought was to drop the whole thing, it seemed not to matter anymore, even to be out of place. But I've thought better of it; Rod thought it was something I should do and I feel I owe it to him, and to you as well, Professor Prye, I know you've spent a lot of time in our behalf. Can you come to my place tomorrow morning about ten? And please bring Mrs. Prye, if she's free, I think she'll be interested in our art collection."

Alice wouldn't have stayed away for all the world. The Richardsons lived in a new apartment tower above the Museum of Modern Art. She had seen the apartment in an interior-design magazine and had found it spectacular. It made an even stronger impression on her when she stood before a giant Alex Katz triple portrait on one of the living room walls, admired a Noguchi bird, and murmured her thanks as John Richardson (his wife was not in view) placed her coffee cup on a granite sculpture that served as a table. "You seem to like my collection, Mrs. Prye," Richardson said, "but I always tell my guests that, if they think this stuff is good, they ought to see what we keep in the basement."

This offhand reference to the Museum of Modern Art had obviously become a cliché, but Richardson still found it hugely amusing. "Well then, how to begin? I can't imagine there's anything I can tell you that hasn't already been dragged out of me by Lieutenant Emmerich."

Richardson spoke between barely parted lips, a mode of upper-class New Yorkese which observers of local mores had dubbed "Locust Valley lockjaw."

"Of course the police are quite properly focusing on Baker's death. It's still the letters that concern you, I gather."

Paul decided on a frontal assault. "I'm afraid that death is my subject too. It didn't start out that way, certainly, when Rodney first showed me the false condolence notes, but that's the way it has turned out. And it's not one death, as I thought I heard you suggest, Mr. Richardson, but two. Surely you have no doubt by now that Mrs. Ackerman was also murdered.

"When I first started looking into this letter business, a lot of people at the club didn't take the matter very seriously. I don't want to be discourteous, but maybe you were one of them. The notes were in poor taste, no doubt of that, but they just didn't seem that important. So people humored me, told me what they wanted to, and some people didn't talk at all. But Rodney for one said something worrisome was going on, and it's tragic, isn't it, he paid for his realism with his life."

Richardson found it easy to drop any pretense of cordiality. "I hear my sermons on Sunday, Professor Prye; it might be better if we got down to business."

Paul retreated from the show of aggression; it was his way. "If I've come on too strong, I apologize, Mr. Richardson, but what I'm saying is this: I believe that Rodney suspected all along that these letters touched on grievances within the inner circles of the club. The circumstances of his death prove him right, don't they? Isn't it apparent that all is not well within the councils of the Oversight Committee?" Paul felt a sense of release in being able to use those words at last in the presence of the club ruler.

"The Oversight Committee is not our term; it's what others call our informal group, but I'll let it pass. Are you telling me that the man who wrote these notes and who murdered Rod Baker is a member of our group?"

"I'm far from being able to say that, but I suspect that Baker's murderer arranged to talk to him before your meeting. Tell me this, if you will, Mr. Richardson. Is it customary for the Oversight Committee to invite outsiders to its meetings?"

"If by outsiders you mean persons who don't usually meet with us—you'll understand that our attendance does vary—I would say it would be most unusual."

"And were there any outsiders invited to Tuesday's meeting?"

"Yes, I've already told the police that Mr. Kennedy was invited to report on Bessarabian Night."

"Including, I suppose, his summary of what information was available concerning Mrs. Ackerman's death."

Richardson was staring at him now. "I expect that was on everyone's mind."

"And what about Baker? Were you to have a report from him as well?"

"Come now, Professor Prye, I don't need to be tested for veracity, it is quite unnecessary. You know better than I that you made some requests of Rod Baker which he agreed to bring before . . . the Advisory Committee. But I will remind you, if you have possibly forgotten, that you wanted us to consider obtaining printing samples from our membership and that you also requested an opportunity to appear before us. He was planning to speak about these two matters at Tuesday's meeting."

Paul was impressed by his own persistence in the face of Richardson's growing opposition. "What else were you planning to take up on Tuesday?"

Richardson raised his voice just enough to make his point. "I hardly think that would concern you or the police, Professor Prye; it had nothing to do with the matters that interest you." He then took a more conciliatory tone. "I can tell you, however, that it would have been a short meeting."

Paul lost his temper, stunning Alice with the abruptness of his reply. "Maybe that's right, Mr. Richardson, and there was nothing more to come before you on Tuesday; but if not on Tuesday, it will be there on another day, won't it, it will not go away. Tell me, Mr. Richardson, before more harm is done: What is on your agenda?"

Richardson flushed and began to rise. But he thought better of it and collapsed into his chair as if relieved to feel pent-up energy flow out of him. He sat in silence for what seemed to Paul to be close to a minute and then said, "Our next meeting is this Saturday at two P.M., in the club library. We will be pleased to have you, Professor Prye, as our guest." He saw them out, saying to Alice as they came into the vestibule, "I hope you didn't miss the Rothko over there. It's an early work, of course, but absolutely rapturous, don't you agree?"

Now I know who he reminds me of, Alice thought. It's the duke in My Last Duchess.

★   ★   ★

Late that night the Pryes called Dave Emmerich.

"I have sort of disappointing news for you," Emmerich reported. "The moles at the bank have taken a run through the depository tonight and have come up dry."

Paul was crestfallen. "Were there boxes then for them to look at? I guess it means that some of the Alumni must have been in there Tuesday afternoon."

"One or two, but nobody whose name has shown up in our investigation yet. But the bank guys were more thorough than that, maybe because they would just as soon help us pin this one on a nonmember. They looked through the boxes of everyone who had access to the vault on Tuesday, club member or not. No silver or other metal objects, tarnishable or not. I guess we figured out that one wrong somehow. Our fellow must have slipped out the bank building's street entrance and disposed of the weapon at his convenience. Some refuse box marked 'Keep New York Clean' probably holds the secret to the crime. Whoops, sorry I said that. Now you're going to suggest we examine every refuse box in the five boroughs."

Paul was depressed when he put down the phone. He said to Alice, "This case is starting to get to me."

"You're close, darling; keep at it."

He looked over to her bed where she lay but realized that he shouldn't expect more than encouraging words. She was reading *W* magazine and dreaming of patterns that had nothing to do with the Alumni Club mystery.

"Alice, would you miss me if I go out for a few minutes?"

"Whatever for? It's awfully late."

"I thought I might be able to get tomorrow's *Times* at the corner."

He brought the paper back and read her the follow-up article he'd expected to find on Baker's murder.

> The police do not report any progress in the investiga-
> tion of the bludgeon murder of Stony Brook mayor

Rodney Baker on Tuesday in a conference room of the Midtown National Bank. Yesterday's report that Mr. Baker was killed shortly before a scheduled meeting of the Alumni Club has now been confirmed. James Preswick, Alumni Club president, issued a statement to the press Thursday evening. Mr. Preswick blamed the crime on what he called "inadequate security measures at the bank that failed to restrict or monitor access from the street to the corridor in which its conference rooms are located." He added that "in the future club meetings will be held either on club premises or in other well-protected locations."

Alice shook her head. "That guy Richardson was conning us, I guess; I thought you'd begun to sell him on the likelihood of an inside job."

CHAPTER 11

"The painters are finished."
Alice had been called away from their breakfast table in the club dining room and now she had returned with the unwelcome news. "They say we can move back home on Monday, if we don't mind breathing through our mouths, like a sweet pair of guppies. Hasn't it all worked out for the best? You'll just have time to make your debut before the Oversight Committee."

"All for the best? It's like the recurring nightmare we both have and all the other walking wounded from America's schools—the one where you show up for the exam in a course where you've never cracked a book. Fine, I've been given the floor, but what do I have to say? How interesting it's all been reading their private correspondence?"

Alice munched a Danish as she prompted him. "I thought you were going to exhort them to turn in their writing samples?"

"That was the plan all right, but it seems sadly out of date now that Baker's been killed. It wasn't a bad idea in its time, though. At least I think it frightened the Friend and made him pretty furious when he couldn't get Rodney to withdraw it. No, I think it's too late for leisurely steps now. I'd like to rise to my feet before all these eminent men and point to the one among them that slugged Rodney and somehow hid his weapon in the depository."

"Have you forgotten what Dave told us about his search there?"

"No, I haven't forgotten, it's just that I can't accept the fact that somewhere I've gone wrong."

Alice continued to nibble the Danish but somewhat more slowly. "Paul," she said, "is it possible that your thinking isn't so much wrong as it is incomplete?"

He looked at her with growing mistrust. Radiant confidence bloomed in her face, as it did when she informed him of one of her triumphs in art scholarship, what she termed a "find" (minor but fascinating discovery) or a "breakthrough" (prophetic revelation).

"What do you have in your hyperactive mind, Madame Mycroft?" he asked her.

"Well, you know how I yield to you in matters of business," she said with gentle mockery, having had to balance his badly snarled checking account on more than one occasion, "so forgive me if I've gone astray. But I had always understood that a safe depository is not the only bank department that takes deposits."

Paul paused long enough to cast her a love-smitten look and jumped to his feet. "My God, you must be right. How long have you been letting me make a fool of myself?"

"Fools, plural," Alice corrected him. "Emmerich prowled the corridor with you stride for stride. But I'm teasing you, you've been quite close all along and I just came up with my little modification on the way back from the phone conversation with the painter. While I was on the line, some joker jostled the door of my booth and the change purse fell out of my bag. When I picked it up, I was impressed how heavy it was."

The Pryes returned to their room and called Emmerich, who found the idea bizarre, but was just about ready to try any lead in the frustrating case. "It's wild," he said, "but how much wilder is it than a flashlight? Did I say that? You guys must be getting to me. I'll be right over."

Paul's next call was to John Richardson. He had two requests. Was there a photographic album of current members? Richardson said there was and that he would arrange for Avery Hopwood, the new associate manager, to lend it to the Pryes. Paul's second request was also granted: Richardson would be glad to see him at his apartment in the afternoon.

By the time Emmerich arrived, Paul had collected an eight-volume set of photographic albums from Hopwood, a humorless young man who looked like a promising replacement for Ross Lytton, and carried them with the doorman's help to Room 759. When the Pryes met Emmerich in the lobby, though, Paul had only one album in his hand. "It's all we need," he told Dave. "I feel as sure of that as I have ever felt of anything in this case."

Alice laughed, remembering all the false starts he had made. Paul backtracked a little. "And if I'm wrong I have seven more volumes up in our room. Dave, can you do your thing again with the Alumni who run the bank?"

The Pryes waited in the lobby while Emmerich placed a call from the parlor. After a few minutes he came back to them, fanning his arms as if practicing the Charleston. They knew the gesture; it meant he had everything arranged. "Are you both pretty brave? A VP's going to meet us in Conference Room A." That was the small conference room where Paul had examined files while an Oversight Committee meeting (he had no doubt now that's what it had been) was in full progress down the hall.

The Pryes walked after Emmerich through the connecting door into the bank. When Dave and Alice turned right into the business corridor, Paul paused for a moment to look over his shoulder at the grille of the safe depository. It was a glance full of nostalgia for a solution that had gone wrong.

After a short wait in Conference Room A, Emmerich and the Pryes were joined by a brisk bank officer who explained the ground rules. He'd send the tellers to them one by one, everyone who'd been on service Tuesday afternoon would be accounted for. But they must agree not to detain the employees long; Friday was always a busy day, especially before a summer weekend.

Paul yielded the lead role to Emmerich, the professional among them. Dave sat at the head of the conference table; Alice moved a chair to one of the side walls and sat trying to look self-absorbed, and Paul hovered over a cold coffeepot at the rear of the room.

Single file the tellers came, most visibly unnerved; they almost wished that they were facing a bank examiner on suspicion of impropriety rather than being summoned, as they knew they were, to furnish evidence about what was to them "the bank murder." Eight tellers were questioned without result; they could not remember any unusually large deposits of coins on Tuesday, and though they peered diligently at the pictures in the album as Emmerich slowly turned the pages, they could not say that on the day of the murder any of the men had appeared before their cages or had been in the bank lobby. Paul fidgeted with the coffeepot; he was just about to decide that his prediction of the murderer's identity had been no more than suspicion after all and that he must return ingloriously for the other seven volumes. But if the tellers couldn't remember the deposit, what would be the use?

The ninth teller was a small, delicately built woman in her fifties. Dave Emmerich, having lost his little faith in Alice's brainstorm, ran through his questions as if they were a tiresome formula.

"Mrs. Keller, is it?"

"Yes," the woman replied with great poise. "Irmgard Keller."

"Mrs. Keller, were you at your cage last Tuesday afternoon?"

"Not all afternoon," the teller said precisely. "I had lunch between one and two. I always return promptly at two; some of our newer people don't care as much about these things, but in my day we were taught to be on time."

"Did you have any breaks in the course of the afternoon?"

"I was entitled to two fifteen-minute breaks, but I didn't take them. We had a lot of customers on Tuesday, I don't know why; but I hate to have them wait." Mrs. Keller seemed to show no awareness that she had landed in the middle of a murder investigation; Alice thought she was acting as if she were singing her own praises to a placement bureau or a bonus committee.

Emmerich pursued his routine questioning. "I understand you must have helped many customers on Tuesday, Mrs. Keller, but I wonder whether you remember receiving a large deposit of coin rolls."

"You mean from bank couriers? We get a pretty good-sized deposit of coins from them, especially if they're coming from retail establishments with video games or food or cigarette dispensers. Of course, sometimes it's the other way around, they run out of pennies or nickels."

"No," Dave said, "that's not what I had in mind; I was thinking of a private depositor, someone who may have had a large load of coin rolls to deposit or exchange for dollars."

The skies cleared for Mrs. Keller. "As a matter of fact, I did have one man come in with quite a lot of rolls. Mostly quarters, you don't see them as much as the smaller stuff. I remember kidding him, telling him I didn't know he worked for the mint."

The Pryes froze as Dave said calmly, "Let me show you this album, Mrs. Keller."

"That's quite unnecessary," she answered. "He's been banking here for years."

Paul joined Alice in their room after lunch.

"I've talked to Richardson again and I've got good news and bad news."

Alice's eyes rolled at her least favorite conversational gambit. "Let's hear it, since there's no escape, but go a little heavier on the vodka this time." She extended her empty glass.

"The good news is that Dave Emmerich is also invited to

tomorrow's meeting of the Oversight Committee. The bad news is you still aren't."

Alice approved the level of his refill and put him at his ease. "Not to worry, there's an antique show in South Street Seaport. And now, if you'll excuse me, one of the Pryes at least is off to work, staggering a little, to be sure, but essentially unbowed. Thanks for lunch."

On her way out of the room she heard Paul begin a telephone conversation. "Mr. Ackerman, I'm glad I caught you in. Listen, I'm sorry to trouble you again, but when you were good enough to ask me over, I think I may have asked you the wrong question. . . ."

Alice was as curious as the next person, probably more so, but, exercising supreme self-control, she quietly closed the door and left him to continue his conversation in privacy. He'd been unusually open about his thought processes in the Alumni Club affair, but he hadn't altogether stopped hoarding his little secrets. Truth to tell, she wouldn't have had it any other way. Surprises were scarcer in the third decade of their marriage.

Paul talked to Ackerman for about ten minutes and made a brief entry in his spiral notebook. He then placed another call, to Vance Parry, but learned that he had left for London. He asked for Marian Morrison, but was told that she was traveling with him. Parry's secretary explained that an annual planning meeting was to be held on Monday at the corporation's English headquarters.

Disappointed, Paul spent a little while reviewing his notes of the case and beginning to sketch out on a lined pad the main points of his presentation to the Oversight Committee. He was soon absorbed in the task, and when he looked up from his writing and consulted his watch, he barely had time to catch a taxi for his appointment with Richardson.

After they had fenced for close to a half hour, Richardson asked abruptly, "You must tell me, Professor Prye, in return for all my indiscreet disclosures, whether you have solved the case."

"Do you mean the case of the anonymous letters?"

"Yes, that, of course," Richardson answered a little uncertainly, allowing control of the dialogue to slip away, "but I'd understood you to say that the mystery of the letters and the murder case were somehow mixed up together."

"And so they are," Paul said. "There's no doubt of that at all."

Richardson was worried. He bit his lip, and the thin stream of his words turned into a hiss. "And do I gather that you and Lieutenant Emmerich have identified the murderer?"

Paul replied with a challenge. "It would be dangerous for you to assume that we have not. You see that now surely, dangerous for you and for the club. And yet I understand your dilemma. You've withheld relevant information, possibly for what you've thought to be the best of motives, and now that it's time to tell, you don't know how."

"Prye, what in the hell are you talking about?"

"I'm talking about the reason Melanie Ackerman and Rodney Baker were murdered. I think you can help us explain why."

Richardson was not so easily bullied. "We're not playing poker, Prye; show me your hand."

Paul took up the gauntlet, and, holding back much that was essential, he laid out an outline of his theory of the club murders. His portrait of the killer was sketchy, leaving much for Richardson to fill in, like the picture games in children's magazines that called for lines to be drawn between consecutively numbered points to form a face.

Richardson did not admit defeat, but after listening without comment, he at last consented to answer the questions that he knew all along Paul had returned to press.

Leaving Richardson's building, Paul hailed a taxi and gave the address of the club. The cab driver didn't disguise his interest: "Isn't that the place where the Stony Brook mayor was bumped off?" When Paul acknowledged that it was, the cabby shared his theory of the case. "It's probably one of those contractor bribery scams. These politicians make millions, and then don't want to divvy up the profit. You know what I mean?"

"Very interesting idea; you really ought to call the police." Paul smiled, hoping that Emmerich would get the call.

Arriving at the club, Paul walked to the reception desk to inquire after messages. Miss Gustave handed him a slip: John Richardson had called a few minutes earlier.

Had the man lied or left out something significant? Paul would not have been surprised in the least, but what would seem out of character was for the man, if he was once resolved on deception, to change his mind; John Richardson did not appear to be a person given to afterthoughts. Paul called him from one of the booths in the front parlor.

Mrs. Richardson answered and put her husband on. "Thanks for calling, Paul," he said. "I've just received some strange news from the club I thought I should pass along to you."

"Yes," Paul responded quietly, letting Richardson set the pace of the conversation.

"You'll recall our talking about the practical jokes that preceded Mrs. Ackerman's death; well, it looks like they've started up again."

"What's happened?"

"Somebody's forced open a cabinet in the library and stolen the club's old voting box."

"When was the theft first discovered?"

"It's Miles Corbett who first noticed the box was missing when he was in the library this afternoon. He's just dropped by to tell me. Why would a man commit two murders, and then relapse into trifles? Any thoughts?"

"None at all," Paul answered. "You're right, it's very strange."

Paul rose slowly through layers of sleep, dreaming that the cycle was beginning again, like the ghost story that always returned to "one dark and stormy night." As his brain cleared he knew what his dream was telling him; the bedside clock read 2 A.M., yet the phone was ringing.

He reached unsteadily for the receiver, preparing himself for a new warning from the club engineer. But he couldn't have been farther from the mark; it was his friend Ben Tolliver calling from Venice. Ben was even worse than Paul with time zones, and in fact his mathematical skills quite exhausted themselves in scanning the blank verse of his beloved Elizabethans.

"'sthat you, Prye? What time is it there?" Tolliver's inquiry was not an apology but a genuine plea for information.

"Forget it, Ben," Paul said crossly. "I'm up. How's Europe?"

"A mixed pleasure this year. Strong men and weak dollars. What can I do for you?"

Paul was still only halfway there. "Have I asked you to do anything?"

"My secretary writes that you called my office."

Another of Ben's social charms was his relaxed attitude towards returning messages.

"Oh, that," Paul lied, "I was going to suggest lunch."

"A great idea; how about Harry's Bar this afternoon?"

Paul attempted a low chuckle but he gave up and settled for clearing his throat.

"Say, what the hell are you doing over there at the Alumni Club? My secretary tells me you've been staying there and suddenly they've got two mysterious deaths. Isn't there a question of your carrying your hobby too far?" He dropped his humorous tone before Paul could answer. "Bad taste, I know, it's been the curse of my life. I'm the last one who should joke about Rod Baker. He was always a great friend."

"Really," Paul said, "I wasn't aware you knew him."

"Didn't I tell you? He was the sponsor of my Alumni Club application. By the way, I don't think I mentioned it to you before I left, but the whole effort turned into a fiasco. Some of the club's prize assholes managed to dredge up my old trials and tribulations at the college. Rod thought we weren't going to make it, so I authorized him to deep-six the application."

"Who was it that opposed your membership?"

Ben laughed. "You knew Rod, soul of discretion, no names, please, that sort of thing. But he made it clear that my application had split the club's officialdom wide open; people were passing each other in the hallways without a word. Rod said the situation was getting out of hand, and I agreed. Especially when he told me that he didn't think he had the votes."

"You mean on the Admissions Committee?" Paul didn't think Ben would notice that the conversation was turning into a civics course.

"That's probably what the rules say should matter, but according to Rod, that's not the way it works. He said he'd taken my application to the club's big shots to see if it would fly, and it didn't, obviously, it fluttered to the ground with a pair of broken wings."

"Is that where the bad blood arose, among the 'big shots'?"

"That's definitely the impression I got from Rod, but as I say, he wasn't the type to mention names and addresses."

Paul turned the conversation to trivia and promised to set up a lunch when Tolliver returned to New York. He sent Alice's love, and she could have confirmed it personally, for she now lay awake on her pillow, extension phone to her ear, as Ben was artlessly adding the final piece to the mosaic of the Alumni Club case.

CHAPTER 12

Paul Prye and Dave Emmerich arrived a little late for the meeting of the Oversight Committee, which was held in the conference room adjoining the club library. John Richardson, who presided, rose to acknowledge their arrival, but all others in attendance remained seated. Paul guessed that their invitation had not been approved unanimously. He saw a few familiar faces around the table; Victor Baines and Miles Corbett sat close to the head of the table and Ralph Murray near the door. Richardson introduced him to the well-suntanned Jim Preswick, the club president, and to a number of other men Paul had not met but whose names he entered at his first opportunity (probably in garbled form) in his notebook.

"You'll excuse us, gentlemen," Richardson said, "we have a little business to complete before we hear from you. You may continue, Harley." A man on Richardson's left took up the thread of a complicated discourse on the club's tax-exempt status.

Paul did not try to follow the speaker's arguments; instead he gazed with anticipation at the wide black briefcase he had set down beside him on the floor. It was as big as at least three dispatch cases and resembled the kind that lawyers use

for closing documents or salesmen carry to transport samples. He was rarely parted from it, even when a more
modest-sized valise would have served just as well. Once he
had been seated in an airport bar, waiting for the plane that
would take him to a speaking engagement in Los Angeles,
when an unattached young woman, eyeing the voluminous
case, had asked him, "What are you selling?" Before he could
retrieve the words, he heard himself say, for all the world as
if he were a boozy hero of Eugene O'Neill or William
Saroyan, "The past, my dear; I'm selling the past."

When the club's tax problems had been resolved for better
or worse, Richardson recognized Paul Prye.

"Professor Prye is next on today's agenda. We have invited
him to our meeting so that he can report to us on the progress
of his investigation. Lieutenant Emmerich is here at Professor Prye's request." Richardson appeared to want very much
to emphasize that it was not his own idea to invite a
policeman into the club's inner sanctum.

Paul thanked him and nudged the chair he had taken closer
to the table. Somehow the exclusivity of the Oversight
Committee had overawed him, in spite of his better judgment, and he felt that to sit shoulder to shoulder with its
membership would be some kind of profanation. He fum-
bled for a moment in a pocket of his jacket and withdrew a
few three-by-five cards to which he had entrusted the
principal points he wanted to make.

"Thank you very much," he said as he worried about how
to start off. He didn't want to antagonize them by coming on
too strong but he had to grab their attention at once and hold
it as he led them in a direction in which they had no wish to
go.

"First of all, gentlemen, my wife and I would like to thank
you and the club for the hospitality you have shown us while
we've been exiled from our home. I'm glad to say that our
painters are now finished and that we're planning to leave
Monday, but you've certainly made us feel at home away
from home." Paul thought that when he left the club he'd
have to take his sincerity in for major repairs.

"It was Rodney Baker, as I think you all know, who asked me to look into the matter of the anonymous letters from the person who signed himself 'a Friend from the Alumni Club.' It seemed a pretty paltry matter at first, but before I knew it I couldn't help seeing that other things were going wrong at the club: someone had tainted the wine with MSG, was rearranging dinner place cards to remind the guests of love affairs that were better left forgotten, and was persistently messing up the squash schedules. All this was pretty malicious and was more than enough in the aggregate to show that somebody was expending a lot of energy venting hostility. But still I wouldn't blame those of you who may have thought it was hardly worth your attention. Maybe I would have ended up thinking so myself if the murders had not come along, but as I see it and have thought for a long time, there is no doubt that the murderer is the same person who played all these mindless tricks on you and other club members.

"I started, as I said, with the letters and tried to figure out who would have a motive to send them to the targets we knew about: Mr. and Mrs. Richardson; you, Mr. Corbett, and Aileen Scroop; Vance Parry and Marian Morrison; and subsequently to the first murder victim, Melanie Ackerman.

"Later my Alice received a letter predicting my own violent death and I was sent an obviously fictitious squash invitation, but I think these were sent on the spur of the moment in the hope of chasing us away from the club. Now who would have written these messages and why? My wife thought that they must have been written by a woman, because in the past women have often expressed aggression through poison pens and indeed through poison as well. I thought Alice was wrong, that times have changed and that women now handle guns and blunt instruments as well as the male sex and have no need for these subtler weapons. But I'm not sure everyone would agree with me in this and I haven't the statistics to prove it. In time I came to the conclusion that the Friend from the Alumni Club was not a woman but that Alice believed what he intended us all to believe. You see, the letters, as those of you who've seen them will know, were noncommittal as to the writer's sex, but the Friend wanted us to conclude that a woman had written them. If you'll pardon me for speaking frankly, the letters to Mrs. Richardson and Aileen Scroop contain hints of their partners' infidelity and suggest that the writer was a woman wronged."

Paul shot a worried look in the direction of Richardson and Corbett to see whether he was treading over the line into impropriety. They did not look at all upset, and Paul pinned his hope on the possibility that even the members of the Oversight Committee had a touch of locker-room bravado. "What bothered me at the start was that the condolence note to Marian Morrison about the death of Vance Parry didn't seem to fit in at all. There was no reference in the letter to other romantic adventures and nobody has suggested to me that that's in the picture." Despite the fact that he'd had smooth sailing so far, Paul hurried quickly through his next comments.

"So I returned to the Richardson and Scroop letters. What woman was the writer trying to impersonate? I settled in time on the possibility that the Friend was pretending to be Melanie Ackerman, whose name has been linked to the two gentlemen in question and," Paul hastened to add, "with many others as well. Of course, I have a healthy skepticism about all this gossip, and its truth may not matter much except as the Friend from the Alumni Club believed it to be true.

"As I said, the Parry letter didn't seem to fit the pattern, so I put it aside for a while only to face a more difficult puzzle, the purpose of the letter to Melanie that she received shortly before her death. She told many stories about the content of this letter but showed it to no one. I think she gave the correct account to Brian Kennedy on Bessarabian Night when she said the letter predicted her death. I believe the very hostility of such a message, and perhaps some personal details as well, tipped her off as to who the writer was. When I first interviewed her husband, I asked a lot of indiscreet questions because he made it pretty clear they had a wide-open marriage. I asked him to name Melanie's lovers at the club and he didn't really help me a great deal. I think he may well have been pretty honest because I suspect that Melanie's reputation as a conqueror of men has been greatly exaggerated. It was only yesterday, in light of all that has happened since, that I realized I had asked Lester the wrong question. It was not, I now believe, one of Melanie's lovers who wrote the first three letters, hoping they would be attributed to her, and capped them with a vicious letter to Melanie herself. I believe that it was a man whose advances were rejected by Melanie with a contempt he could not erase from his mind.

"When Melanie received the letter from him, she was furious. She arranged a private meeting with him on the gallery on Bessarabian Night after she had reenforced her nerves at the bar. He took Lester's flashlight from her to lead the way to a secluded area of the gallery, struck her with it and pushed her over the balustrade. I do not think he intended to kill her when he agreed to the meeting. But I believe he is a man who finds it difficult to control his temper under stress, and when she threatened to unmask him as the Friend from the Alumni Club, I think he could not face the loss of his position and indeed his membership at the club.

"Of course, when Melanie died I did not know the identity of her murderer, and although my suspicions increased I could not have named him with certainty until yesterday. And I still had to figure out why the murderer had written to Marian Morrison and what the point was of all his other antics at the club. If Lieutenant Emmerich were not sitting at my side to restrain me, I could tell you a little about the Molineux murder case that focused on the Knickerbocker Club in this city around the turn of the century. Suffice it to say that many of us believe that Molineux's attacks on the lives of two club members were motivated both by rivalry in love and hostility to what he regarded as the lowering of the club's administrative standards.

"I wondered whether this second element was also at play here. After all, the Friend's letters (except the one to Melanie) attacked prominent clubmen. As I put the Friend's dirty tricks side by side, they seemed at first to have no connection with each other, but in time they assumed a pattern. The pattern was one of protest against club policy and, more important, it was not the protest of a reformer but the indignant cry of a conservative. The conservative I envisioned was a man who believed that a club which for years had served the best vintages should not lower itself to purchasing bulk regionals of doubtful quality. He was outraged at what he regarded as a debasement of the club's admissions standards, unwritten as they were for the most part. It was his objection to the great increase in membership in recent years that prompted him to mix up the squash appointments, hoping to suggest that there were now too many people to be accommodated efficiently on the courts.

"Many of the individual decisions of the Admissions Committee made him frantic. It is my surmise that he was opposed to the admission of Tom Simmons and that he may also have abetted the rejection of the candidacy of my good friend, Ben Tolliver. But I am convinced that the event that infuriated him unbearably, and may have triggered his entire terror campaign, was what he saw as a major blunder of the Admissions Committee in approving the candidacy of an impostor who called himself Charlie Benson the Fourth. Shortly after the public posting of Benson's expulsion, the Friend's letters began to arrive in the mail."

Paul headed with caution towards the main goal of his analysis.

"There was, in addition to all these cumulating grievances, another source of unquenchable rage at the club fathers. I believe the Friend is a man who holds that the downfall of the Alumni Club dates from its decision to admit women. Melanie Ackerman, I understand, was one of the first female graduates accepted for membership. When she was admitted and he heard more and more about her rumored conquests at the club, he felt confirmed in the rightness of the cause he had supported—and I suppose he felt even more indignant when it seemed that Melanie was prepared to say yes to all male members except him. I think it was his opposition to women's membership that gave him the idea of impersonating a female poison-pen letter writer and also suggested the trick of scrambling the place cards at the new members' dinner to suggest the hanky-panky that had resulted from female intrusion.

"These speculations brought me back to the Friend's letter to Marian Morrison, who was not known, like Melanie Ackerman, for alleged promiscuity, but for the fixed determination of Vance Parry to promote her in the male world in the face of gossip. Parry's sponsorship of Ms. Morrison would have been enough to make the Friend dislike him, but was it sufficient cause to make him and his protégée the targets of a poison-pen letter? I thought not and only recently have I learned (from which among you is not important) what galled the Friend about Parry and what turned him against many of you gentlemen as well. I am informed that for several months now, amidst bitter debate, you have had on your agenda the proposal of Vance Parry, the most generous financial backer of the club, that Marian Morrison be admitted as the first female member of the Oversight Committee."

Paul paused to observe several exchanges of recriminating looks around the table.

"Frankly, I wish I had been told of that a good deal earlier, or that you had entrusted your closely guarded secret to Lieutenant Emmerich. I think that had we known that, the life of Rodney Baker might have been spared. It is my information that Mr. Baker was inclined to favor the candidacy of Ms. Morrison, as I know he sponsored the admission application of Ben Tolliver against heavy odds. I believe that when Baker announced an intention to present my request that this committee embark on a campaign to obtain printing samples from five hundred members—beginning most likely with those of this committee—the Friend arranged to see Baker in Conference Room B right before your meeting was to begin. When he was unable to shake Baker's intention to push that proposal or his equal determination to continue deliberation on the Morrison candidacy, the Friend lost his temper and struck Baker down with a heavy object nearest at hand."

After relishing a roomful of puzzled looks, Paul recounted the results of the interviews at the bank, withholding only the name of the customer Mrs. Keller had given them.

"Does that complete your report?" Ralph Murray asked with a show of impatience. "We do have some other items on the agenda, I believe, John."

Dave Emmerich began to rock in his chair.

"Not quite," Paul answered. "Please bear with me for a few more minutes and I will be done."

Paul welcomed Murray's interruption and let a long silence work its unsettling effect on the committee. He scanned the conference table from end to end as if he were memorizing the order in which the members sat, and then laughed with perhaps even more artifice than he had counted on. "I've been throwing a lot of accusations around, so I shouldn't spare myself entirely." He reached down, unclasped his briefcase, and set upon the table the club's missing voting box.

The box had double hinges that permitted its lid to be raised so as to provide access to either of the two compartments into which it was divided. In the compartment near the rear of the box (which was fitted with a turned wooden handle) an ample supply of white and black marbles was stored. When the lid of this storage chamber was raised and pushed back on its hinges, side panels with high triangular projections emerged to screen the hand of the voter from view. A vote was cast by choosing a ball and pushing it through a funnel-shaped hole in the box's partition into the voting compartment. After everyone had voted, the lid of the voting compartment would be raised so that the result of the election could be determined.

"It wasn't exactly theft," Paul said, "I assure you of that, and how could I say anything else in the presence of my friend, the policeman? Let's call it instead a borrowing without advance authorization. I'm sure, though, you will approve my purpose when you hear me out.

"But first you must let me tell you a story about a club member's election. It is from the eighteenth century, but you'll forgive me for that, I know; after all, I am a historian.

"The man I want to tell you about had a temper as bad as the Alumni Club murderer, maybe worse, in fact. His name was George Robert Fitzgerald, but he was involved in so many duels he was known as Fighting Fitzgerald. He applied for membership in London's famous Brooks's Club, and when the admission committee voted he was blackballed unanimously. The trouble was, though, that nobody was enthusiastic about being delegated to report the result to Fitzgerald, who was waiting downstairs, for fear of being challenged to a duel on the spot. When Brooks himself finally mustered the courage to bring him the bad news, Fitzgerald burst into the clubroom in defiance of all rules and forced the committee members to announce their votes individually. Needless to say, he was admitted to membership without dissent.

"Now, why do I trouble you with clubland's ancient lore? Because I've felt from the start of my investigation that the ghost of Fighting Fitzgerald has been glaring over my shoulder. Many of you must have suspected that all was not well within your ranks, and some, I feel sure, must have known who among you was most bitterly opposed to changes in your policies. But you didn't tell me, hoping against hope, with Rodney Baker, that I'd find some more palatable explanation for the letters and the other dirty tricks. As the tricks were followed by violence, your suspicions must have turned in time to near certainty, but still you kept silent, thinking you were protecting the honor of the club's name.

"So I propose now to reverse the strategy of Fighting Fitzgerald, and to ask of you as a group the judgment you have refused to give me as individuals."

Paul looked around the table again, but the Oversight Committee remained impassive. He was impressed by their fortitude but nevertheless resumed the explanation of his plan. "I've written the name of my candidate for Alumni

Club murderer on slips of paper that I will distribute to each of you, duly folded. I'll ask you to read the name, reflect on it but remain silent. And after you've had time to deliberate, I'll pass around the voting box. Have you forgotten how to use it? I think not. If you agree that I've picked the right man, just push a black ball into the voting compartment, or a white ball if you think he's innocent."

Paul handed out the slips and waited. The members opened the slips, quickly raised their eyes again, and gazed stonily at Paul. Nobody spoke. Then the voting box went around the room and came back to Paul, who placed it in the middle of the table.

Beckoning to Emmerich to look with him, Paul opened the voting compartment. He counted fourteen balls, all black.

There were fifteen members at the meeting and only one had not voted. Everyone in the room was looking at him. He had placed his hands before him on the table, palms upward in a gesture of concession.

It was Victor Baines. A true parliamentarian of the old school, he had abstained.

Epilogue

Paul interrupted his footnotes on the case to hand Alice her second vodka and give himself a generous refill of Scotch. As she sipped, he looked, probably for the last time, at the photograph that showed the wrong Benson running for a touchdown against Yale in 1916. He wondered idly what had happened to the young man; whether he'd survived World War I; and whether the preserved moment of (what had the book called it?) "gridiron glory" had been the high point of his life. Alice called him back to the present:

"Paul, can I drag you away from football history—where I know your heart really lies? You were about to tell me how you came to suspect that Victor Baines wrote the condolence notes."

Paul didn't want to overstate his foreknowledge. "I'm not sure I'd really picked him out definitively until the bank teller gave us his name. I had so many successive candidates for 'Friend from the Alumni Club,' I can't even recall when Baines became my leading contender. There seemed to be so little enthusiasm around here for my investigation, it didn't take me long to become suspicious of everybody.

"But there was one thing that particularly bothered me about Baines: he never wanted to meet me in any place where we could be alone or where we'd have enough privacy for me to question him closely."

Alice was surprised. "What about Richardson? He didn't want to meet you at all."

Paul acknowledged the point. "That worried me, too, but I thought Richardson, as club potentate, probably felt the whole business was too petty to deserve his notice. By the time I met him, his concerns ran deeper.

"But Baines took a different line. He pretended to cooperate, but kept me on a tight rein. Our first meeting was in a large cocktail lounge that was virtually empty. We could have sat anywhere, but Baines took a seat at the bar where our words could be overheard, or we would worry about being overheard by the only other customer in the place.

"The same thing happened when Baker persuaded him to turn over the files on the room renovation. He managed to deliver his file when Ralph Murray was along and conversation would not be easy."

Paul passed to another point. "Then, too, I suspected that he had stripped the file."

Alice protested. "And didn't Murray? I understood he just gave you summaries and statistics."

"Very true, but at least he was consistent in withholding raw data, ostensibly to protect confidentiality. Baines, on the other hand, gave me original letters and memoranda but he did it on a curious selective principle, namely, that none of them was authored by him. I wondered whether Baines was unwilling for me to see his signature, for fear that his cursive and printing styles had some damning resemblance.

"I also thought the man had lied to me on at least one occasion. His original plan had been to make us all think that the Friend was a woman. After all, aren't most poison-pen letters supposed to come from women?"

Alice looked uncomfortable but hoped it didn't show. Paul didn't press his little victory but continued:

"Nevertheless, he was a very flexible man. When he realized I was looking for a tie between the Benson affair and the origin of the anonymous-letter campaign, he saw both danger and opportunity. There was danger if I stumbled on the truth, that his anger over the Admissions Committee's blunder was what finally kicked off his guerrilla war against the club administration. The opportunity he saw in my investigation was to divert the direction of suspicion: if I didn't fall for the invitation to 'look for the woman,' why not persuade me to suspect the false Benson of writing the letters in revenge for his expulsion? So he fed me the fake line about spotting 'Benson' in the club during the months when the letters were being written. Nobody Emmerich or I talked to confirmed that story, and it seemed improbable on its face.

"When Melanie was killed, I had trouble visualizing Baines as her murderer. But isn't that always true with middle-class murderers? I still can't believe that Tom Simmons, crude as his party manners may be, polished off his wife with a magnum. But when it came to the second murder, and when you first proposed the alternative theory that the weapon had been a bag of coins, a trivial detail I remembered brought Baines to the fore again. I thought of our meeting in the hotel lounge, and how, when our conversation was over, Vic studied our small bill with almost passionate attention and then suggested we split it down the middle. Such a man, it seemed to me, might well be sufficiently compulsive and parsimonious to collect rolls of small change for delivery to his bank." He improvised a refinement to his thought. "At the same time he could be sufficiently sensitive about his hoarding instinct that he would carry his coins in a silver bag."

Alice knew that he had more to say; she chewed on the ice at the bottom of her glass and waited.

"There was something else that I suppose was in the picture from the beginning; he reminded me of Thackeray."

It wasn't what she had expected. "Give me a break," she said, "a plump little Thackeray with a meerschaum."

Paul grinned. "It wasn't that he looked like Thackeray. But I kept thinking of Thackeray's troubles at the Garrick Club. The 'little G.,' he called it, 'the dearest place in all the world.' Thackeray's wife was mad, you know, he had to put her away, and the club meant more to him than any home he could claim elsewhere. So when Edmund Yates broke the unwritten rules by publishing a defamatory article based on Thackeray's club conversations, the gentle giant turned the Garrick topsy-turvy trying to get rid of the young upstart.

"I felt that a similar sense of injustice had warped Baines's perspective. He was a widower and I think he lived for the club alone; he'd become a permanent fixture on the House Committee. Remember Bainesgate? What he saw as an abandonment of standards—the entry of women, the relaxation of admissions criteria, yes, even the serving of bulk wines—all of this was more than he could take lying down."

"But what could he have hoped to accomplish?" Alice asked. "Most of the people we met jeered at the Friend's letters."

"That's what's so sad about it all," Paul agreed. "He was battling in vain against the tides of change. But I'm not sure he cared about failure or saw clearly the end of his struggles. Do you suppose that terrorists dream of a peaceful old age?"

Two days later the Pryes were preparing to leave the Alumni Club and return to Riverdale. Alice had celebrated the grand event by buying a new toaster on her way back from work on Friday. When she presented the appliance to Paul at dinner, he also had a parcel for her: a gift-wrapped bottle of Barolo, which, he assured her, the wine merchant had promised to be free of MSG.

Their bags now stood at the porter's desk, tartan cheeks puffed out to the danger point by the addition of Alice's purchases during their stay. Paul, without excessive nostalgia, left his room key at the desk with the formidable Miss Gustave. Though Paul straightened his tie ostentatiously to show how much he had learned of the proprieties during his brief residence, he could not draw a smile from her stern lips.

When he told Alice how obdurately Miss Gustave had resisted his last desperate attempt at cordiality, Alice sprang to her defense.

"You know that I'm the last person in the world to be competitive, so it is only in the interest of historical truth that I confess to you that Miss Gustave seems to dislike me less than you. She was positively chatty when I came down this morning to surrender my key. Speaking of history, she even told me a little tidbit of club lore that's probably evaded you. Do you know about the ugly past of the joggers' door?"

"No," Paul admitted, "though I'd be glad to learn that joggers were not a part of God's original plan and that they had no place in the architectural drawings of Stanford White."

"You're quite right on both accounts. In the bad old days before women were permitted to use the front door, the joggers' door was the ladies' entrance."

Alice also told Paul that the doorman was nowhere to be found. "Shall we hunt for a cab?" she asked. He nodded, but then had a second thought. "Could you wait just a second?"

He burrowed in a giant soft-sculptured Heineken's beer can that he used as a travel bag, and took out his Polaroid camera. "I'd like to take a few pictures of the Great Hall for my crime files." Alice followed him through the swinging doors into the grillroom and past the Bainesgate archway beyond that led to the Hall. Paul turned to his left and raised his head, searching out the place on the gallery from which Melanie Ackerman had fallen.

"Don't you think it was closer to the writing desk?" Alice suggested. "I think that's where Melanie was leading him, don't you, probably hoping he'd start sweating even before she confronted him with her suspicion. Couldn't she have seen him writing there, maybe more than once, and wondered why he did his correspondence at the club? When she got his condolence note and recognized his printing (and even more clearly his malice), the images of Baines at the desk may have popped back into her mind."

Paul didn't answer immediately because he had just snapped his first picture of the gallery and was waiting for it to develop. Satisfied with the result, he said without turning back to her, "That possibility had never occurred to me. I thought they both had just chosen a convenient dark place for their rendezvous, but your idea adds something almost gothic to the scene. Whether it's true or not, when I lecture to my book club about the case, I'll end with your brilliant conjecture, with full attribution, of course."

"Attribution is the least you owe me," Alice said pettishly, "considering that my figure, which you've been known to praise from time to time, bars me from admission to the hallowed halls of your club."

Paul set out to persuade her of the wrongheadedness of her grievance. "You don't really want to be admitted to a men's club. Look what happened to poor Melanie. But I'll grant you this, we certainly want to illustrate the power of your imagination by getting a shot of the desk." He began to train the camera on his new target, when he was stopped by a club waiter who blocked his camera with one hand and, with the other, proffered one of the notice cards that were placed on the tables of the public rooms. On the other side from the strong warning against the display of public papers, the Pryes read:

> No photographs, whether still or moving, shall be taken, or video camcorders used, in any part of the Club for any purpose whatsoever, without the approval of the House Committee.

"Objection noted," Paul said to the waiter, "but how do you go about getting permission when the head of the House Committee is in jail?"

When they were in their cab, Alice said, "It's just like the lady in the green hat." They both laughed. It was one of their favorite jokes and their experience at the Alumni Club had given it new meaning. During their years at Harvard they had bought a volume of classic cartoons from the *Crimson*. One of them commemorated a successful bank robbery in Harvard Square right under the nose of a traffic cop stationed in a corner kiosk. The cartoon showed an appalling wave of robbery, murder, and rape proceeding unimpeded in the square while the traffic cop bawled obliviously over his loudspeaker: "Will the lady in the green hat please step back to the curb."

"It is a lot like that," Paul said, and, unknowingly repeating a comment Brian Kennedy had made earlier that summer when Tom Simmons was considered for membership, he added: "The club rule book prohibits everything but murder."

"Don't worry, darling," Alice consoled him. "I have boundless faith in the Oversight Committee; they'll add a new rule in the next edition."